Unrecognised Potential

Ravi Kumar R

First published in India 2011 by **Frog Books**
an imprint of **Leadstart Publishing Pvt Ltd**
1 Level, Trade Centre
Bandra Kurla Complex
Bandra (East) Mumbai 400 051 India
Telephone: +91-22-40700804
Fax: +91-22-40700800
Email: info@leadstartcorp.com
www.leadstartcorp.com / www.frogbooks.net

Editorial Office:
Unit: 25-26 / Building A/1
Ground Floor, Near Wadala RTO
Wadala (East) Mumbai 400 037 India
Phone: +91-22-24036548 / 24036930

Sales & Marketing Office:
Unit: 122 / Building B/2
First Floor, Near Wadala RTO
Wadala (East) Mumbai 400 037 India
Phone: +91-22-24046887

US Office:
Axis Corp, 7845 E Oakbrook Circle
Madison, WI 53717 USA

ISBN 978-93-81115-28-2

Publisher and Managing Editor: Sunil K Poolani
Books Editor: Sai Prabha Kamath
Design Editor: Mishta Roy

Typeset in Book Antiqua
Printed at Repro India Ltd, Mumbai

Price — India: Rs 95; Elsewhere: US $6

to the 'thinking' rich and the 'fate-less' poor

About the Author

Ravi Kumar R was born and brought up in Hyderabad, Andhra Pradesh, where he did his entire schooling. He graduated in 2009 from IIT Kharagpur with a B Tech in Electrical Engineering.

He is presently working as an Engineer in BHEL, RC Puram unit, Hyderabad.

Ravi can be contacted at ravirenus@gmail.com

1

Sachin and the Girl in Alpha

Indians love watching cricket. Hyderabadis love it watching in a café. Like any other day during the match, Alpha was crowded with people glued to the television screen. The over-enthusiastic crowd, their language and emotions conveyed that the match was between India and Pakistan.

"Maaki kir kiri, one more wicket down," said Ismail Bhai, the most famous among the group, whose sole purpose was to pass time by gathering a group of youngsters similar in aims and aspirations like him and enlightening them with the experience that he-attained all through his age. Children liked him very much for all the good stories he told them, though it was only later in their life that they learned the truth about the stories. He was very proud of his city and felt that it was better than Rome or London. In the stories he usually created, he utilized the world and Indian history according to his requirements to finally conclude that Hyderabad had given the world everything.

Beside him was Salim, a youngster in his early 20s,

who was almost like a disciple to Ismail Bhai, from whom he had learnt the art of drinking chai to feel it tastier. The size of the group varied depending on the situation, but these two were to be found most of the time in the café.

"Ismail Bhai, did you observe the girl?" said Salim, pointing out his finger towards to the television.

"Kyaa re, kaun re," responded Ismail Bhai impatiently.

"Cameraman has got a devil inside him, Bhai. He is always focusing the girl in red T-shirt. This is the fifth time he has focused on her."

Ismail had a glimpse of the girl in the television and said with a smile that revealed three-fourth of his teeth, "Uski maaki, she is damn hot. She is very excited that we lost the wicket."

"Bhai, won't her parents reprimand her if she wore those kind of dresses?"

"We used to make sound while sipping chai and people used to be irritated. Didn't they get used to us? It is the same way with the parents too. They tell them once or twice. When they don't heed, they leave it to them. Everywhere freedom for the individual is increasing and is given more importance."

"I understood, Bhai."

"Let me tell you one more thing, Salim. In the crowd, there will definitely be many girls who will be better than this girl, but right now, the cameraman has been attracted only to her. His mind, at present is concerned only about her and is looking for opportunities to have a look at her. If there is a wicket or a sixer, see how he focuses her again. It's all in the mind and we just can't leave the thing we are infected with."

As a six was hit, the cameraman focused the girl again and the surprised Salim asked, "How were you able to guess it?"

Ismail Bhai gave a smile that revealed to everyone who knew him that he was going to start a story and said, "I have been watching cricket since Gavaskar was wearing a chaddi. I know all the cameramen and the umpires."

"Bhai, did you really watch Gavaskar play? I mean, not in the television," asked Salim, confused whether he could convey what he actually wanted to ask Ismail Bhai, who had already travelled long back in time.

"It's not just Gavaskar, my dear. Azharuddin, Viswanath, Kapil Dev and a few others whom you might not even know, used to play in our Gymkhana grounds. We won the World Cup long back and there were full celebrations near Charminar and we had great fun. Kapil Dev came to meet his fans waving his hands like the way Nehru did when we got Independence. It's here in this very café, we had congratulated him. Maaki kir kiri, those were the days. Now-a-days, no cricketer cares for the fans... we are the ones who care for them."

Everybody listened to Ismail Bhai interestingly, imagining all that was supposed to have happened in the café long back.

"Bhai, since when was cricket played? When did Indians start playing?" asked Salim.

"You have asked the best question one can ever ask, Salim. Cricket is very old and at that time, neither you nor I was born. The British used to play it in their land. My sixth sense sometimes suggests that they have been inspired from our own games. When they were here in India, those white fellows had nothing to do since they didn't know any of our games and so started playing cricket to show us that they too have games to play. The game was strange but, in a way, similar to our gilli danda with both the sizes of gilli and danda enlarged and so we used to look at the strange enlarged version of our game curiously when they were playing. They used to play it near the Mozamzahi market where our people sell vegetables. They wanted to build a stadium there and so thought of raising the taxes from people, who sold vegetables in the market. We opposed their views, but they never listened to us except occasionally when we praised them. As the arguments grew, they insulted us saying that we were fit for nothing except working in the fields and regarding cricket, they concluded that we weren't even fit to see the game. Then my dad, who was a core committee member of the market, was enraged by their words and challenged them for a match. My dad and many others near Charminar formed a team, played the match and won it . That was the most exciting match I had ever seen. You should have seen the effort all the women and children put in for our men to win the match. It was one of the most cherishable moments in my life. In this process, my dad and mom fell in love with each other and I am the witness for cricket in India. This is how Indians started playing cricket," said Ismail, wiping out the tears that never came from his eyes.

"How did you see the match? You weren't born then?" asked Salim.

"Did I say you that way? It was by mistake. I just heard the story from elders. It keeps running in my mind all the time and so I might have said as if I had seen the match," said Ismail Bhai.

"Anyway, it reminds me of Aamir Khan in Lagaan while hearing this story of your dad, Bhai," said Salim.

"All the films are inspired from the real life stories, bevakoof. Now shut your mouth and watch the match," said Ismail.

"What a shot! See how the ball has crossed the boundary line like a rocket!"

"Ismail Bhai, again the same girl, now she seems to be so sad. Even though she is sad, she is very cute, Bhai."

"If Sachin plays the shot, what else can you expect from the opponent?"

*****

Just in front of the café, there were a few tables and Siddharth sat on the corner table that gave him glimpses of both the inside view of the café and the outside view of the pavement where people strolled. Amidst the unconscious driving flavor of the Irani chai, he loved watching people of different diversities which Hyderabad has attracted and absorbed since centuries. There were young girls wearing jeans and churidars, women wearing saris in different styles; Andhra, Gujarati, Rajasthani, Kashmiri, Marwari, Bengali; vast number of Muslims moving confidently in their proud city. There were old people in dhotis and traditional dresses ready for their evening walks and yoga classes; students with iPods in their ears staring at the film posters on the wall, foreigners who had descended to pursue their internships in the Hitec City, quite amused at the way people here cross the busy traffic roads. Businessmen in cars returning from their workplace surrounded by beggars for a rupee or two as soon as the red lights are on. Like every other city in India, Hyderabad also pays homage to thousands of homeless beggars who come to the city in the hope of earning a livelihood. The beggars seem to be content with their lives. They didn't know the political rights the constitution had granted them, the economic equality which our directive principles had laid down as the objective to the government policies... not even one question came in their minds as to why they were on the streets while a section of people were in air-conditioned cars on the same street at the same time. All they knew was to beg and just beg. Then there were saadus, the traffic police, rickshaw-pullers, auto-wallahs and many other sorts of people.

Like the stars that faded at the sight of the moon, all the people in the surrounding faded out with the appearance of a Muslim girl, coming towards the café. She was young, maybe around 18 years old. She was fully covered in burkha except her eyes. Siddharth's eyes fell on her. As she approached him, he could see her clearly. After observing her eyes carefully for quite some time, he somehow felt that that she was not happy and was worried about something.

Are the Eamcet results out? Is she worried about the huge competition in the exam she is going to appear? Is she unemployed? Is she worried about the studies of her younger siblings? Is she in love with a Hindu guy? Is her engagement fixed against her will? Is she not allowed to go to a movie or tour with her friends? Is she teased by some bunch of rogues near the bus stop? These never-ending list of problems faced by an average Indian girl filled his brain. "How many problems can I think of? After all, how many problems does an Indian girl have?" he thought.

Siddharth was still observing the girl who was now close to him. "Maaki kir kiri! One more wicket down," Ismail Bhai screamed due to which the attention of the girl turned towards the crowd watching the television in the café. She approached the crowd and looked at the television. The score was 151/6 and there was a long way to go for the Indians to win the match. Now that she was very close to him, Siddharth could observe the growing worry in her eyes as she looked at the television for score. Suddenly some text scrolled at the bottom of the television but due to the crowd, she was not able to read it. She leaned forward with her eyes fully open revealing her round black eye balls magnified in beauty because of the beautifully-decorated eye lashes. As she read the required run rate as 8, her wide eyes now began closing down like a full moon to a half moon in a flash of a second. All her frustration and loss of hope was clearly visible in that moment. In her desperation, she turned around to move away from the crowd when she heard someone from the crowd screaming 'Sachin.' That one word lifted her spirits and like a flash, she moved towards the television. She saw Sachin on the screen batting and all of a sudden, there was a glow in her eyes, the glow that made her forget for that instant, all her worries she had. The glow added more beauty to her eyes and made her eye lashes fade away. Siddharth felt he could never forget this glow for the rest of his life.

"Ismail uncle, Sachin is still batting and the required run rate is just 8. You need not worry even if the run rate is above 12. He is on 82 right now. Let him complete 100 and the Pakistanis will see what real cricket is," said the girl.

"Haan beta, Sachin is there in the crease and that is the reason why we still have the hope. The whole fear is that if Sachin goes by any chance, the entire Indian wall collapses. Since you have told it beta, Allah might have heard and he will see that India shall surely win," said Ismail, looking at the girl and smiling to her sweetly.

She started moving away from the crowd and Siddharth could now see her back. Though he could not see her eyes now, he could not forget her eyes and the eye dynamics he witnessed minutes ego. "Eyes say it all, they say. Is this it? All of a sudden, how could she forget the worries she had before though it was for a few seconds? What role did Sachin play? Can I play the role of Sachin to her? Can I become Sachin to all the miseries of the world? How can I contribute myself to wipe out all the tears in the world? What should I do? The role played by Sachin is for a few minutes, how can the duration be increased? Everyone should definitely have Sachin-like figures in their life which makes them forget all their worries. It might be their husband, lover, child, friend, God, garden, country or anything for that matter. How does one realize the significance of the same? Can I play a role in it? Will the busy modern world give me an opportunity or will I perish in my search to find it? Can I become a reason for glow in everyone's face or should I stick only to my Swetha."

The sun moves brother, the sun moves
In both the cases of sunshine and sunset
In the former, it guides us to light
But to darkness in the latter
Tears flow brother, tears flow
In both the cases of sadness and happiness
Till now, they have flown for the darkness
But from now, they flow only to make you glow

The Routine
Get-Together

Siddharth was still sitting in the café which was now fully crowded as the match was getting more interesting. His thoughts were sweeping across all the regions, religions and cultures like the travelling clouds, observing people walking on the road. The clouds stop suddenly at a place observing the uneven patterns. For quite some time, he began to think about a problem and tried to get a solution. Then, he doubted his own ability and finally began to wonder whether he will be able to do it, when the big names like Marx and Gandhi couldn't do it.

It was then that Swetha, the sweetheart of the gang, arrived. She was 23, had a light brown complexion, wearing blue jeans with a white top, she was quite modern in her looks without any makeup except for the kajal around her eyes. Her face was quite charming with a natural appeal and her manners so convincing that she made everyone feel her as a good acquaintance in their first meeting itself. As soon as she arrived, Surya and Imran, both as old as Siddharth and Swetha, joined them from the other end.

"Hello Aristotle, where are you? With Marx or Tolstoy?" asked Swetha, catching the hair of Siddharth to disturb its well-arranged pattern and as Siddharth looked at her, she continued with a calm expression, "I am sorry Siddharth, I kept you waiting. The bus was late as there were continuous traffic jams all along the highway." She sat on the chair beside Siddharth and looking back waving her hand said, "Namasthe, Ismail uncle. What is the status? Is Sachin still batting?"

"Haan beta. By Allah's grace, Sachin is still there and is in good form. He is on 98, but there are only 3 wickets remaining."

"Don't worry, uncle. Sachin is still there. We will definitely win."

Ismail Bhai gave an agreeing smile for what his young friend told him.

"Chotu, one biryani please," said Imran.

Surya looked at Imran, gave a smile that indicated he was going to tell something funny about Imran and said, "Imran has started his eating machine again and so we can ignore him now. I don't know how Nasreen is going to feed him in future."

"Teri maaki, why do you bring Nasreen in every topic that we discuss? Should I call Ismail Bhai and ask him to deliver a lecture on Hyderabad?" asked Imran, tasting the just-arrived biryani.

"Why are you guys late?" enquired Swetha and without waiting for Surya and Imran to answer continued, "You might have been after some girl, right?"

Siddharth gave a smile as if he knows the future course of action that is going to take place while Swetha looked at Surya and asked, "Who is the new girl?"

"Girl!" exclaimed Surya with his face like a kid who was caught stealing by his mother and continued, "there is nothing like that. Why do you always associate me with a girl? Can't I stay without one? I am innocent and not like your Siddharth. He acts innocent but does everything when you are away."

"You need not advise me about Siddharth. I know everything about him. Tell me the reason why you are late?"

"Siddharth is the new Ram avatar and so will never be after any girl except you, the great Sita Devi. We are like the Raavan, who are after all the girls in the street," said Surya and then turned towards Imran and said, "Sorry, Imran. I don't know a Muslim figure who was after girls and so compared you also with Raavan."

"Forget Muslim figures. You don't even know the most basic Hindu personalities and the Raavan comparison too no way suits you. Raavan was after only one woman and is much better than you," said Swetha looking at Surya lifting her eyebrows.

"You should thank me for that. If I should be after only one woman and in case Siddharth is Ram, I should kidnap you as you are Sita," said Surya lifting his eyebrows twice.

"What a great discovery!" exclaimed Swetha stretching her lips as far as she could and said, "Don't change the topic now. Tell me, where have you been? I am not going to leave you until you give me the answer."

"My cousin, who came from the US, had to shop and unfortunately I had to accompany her. I hate to shop with girls for all the experience I have obtained by accompanying you. Moreover, she has just arrived from the US. The mere thought of spending hours and hours in the mall on a Monday frightened me. So, I invited Imran promising him a chicken pizza in return. Then I realized how short your shopping duration is and how simple you are compared to her. I couldn't feed Imran further and so returned asking her to come here. Twenty minutes ago, I called her when she said she will be here in a moment and I am still wondering what the duration of a 'moment' is in a girl's dictionary!"

"So Imran, should I trust what all he has said? Is it really the cousin or something else?"

"Everything he said is true except the pizza part. I ate only one. Shopping with her is really painful. She has seen around 20 brands just for a lipstick," said Imran.

"I can't believe you guys. You know, Siddharth, what this fellow has done to my friend last weekend. He took her to Tank Bund."

As she proceeded further, Surya screamed, "God! Did she tell you everything?"

"Yeah, she told me everything. It was so exciting that I have noted down everything she had told me on a paper," said Swetha and continued, "He took her to the Tank Bund and composed a poem then and there."

"Swetha, please don't tell them," pleaded Surya, but Swetha opened a note from her purse and with a shine over her face said, "He looked closely in to her eyes and said 'till the last second, I sacrificed everything to look at Lord Buddha, but right now, at this moment, I sacrificed Lord Buddha to look at you since you are important to me than Buddha.' "

Hearing this, everyone burst out into laughter, Siddharth placing his hand over stomach while laughing and Imran almost falling down while laughing.

"How did you come up with this beautiful idea of comparing the girl with Lord Buddha?" asked Swetha.

"It is my own idea. I won't copy ideas from anyone. The only clue I got is from an article which suggested that to impress a girl you need to show her that she is most important to you than anything else in the world."

"So you applied it to Gautama Buddha?" asked Siddharth, still unable to control his laughter.

At this moment, Surya's cousin, very fair in complexion and almost their age, came and said, "Hi guys! I guess you are having a very good time."

"Yes! For the last one moment, we are having lots of fun," said Surya stressing the word moment.

"Sorry, dear. I had to shop many things and so it consumed much time."

"Oh yeah, many things in this small cover, right?" asked Imran sarcastically for which she smiled and introduced herself to the gang, "My name is Akanksha. I am this idiot's cousin," pointing to Surya.

"Akanksha, a very good name. You were born and brought up in the US, but your name is still a traditional Indian one. Good to hear that. Do you know its meaning?" asked Siddharth looking at Akanksha.

"No, I guess."

"It means 'desire'."

"Oh, I didn't know that," said Akanksha, staring at Siddharth for a while continuously as if she knew him for a long time.

"Desire... wah, wah... what a great name you have got? I am surprised that we didn't have any discussion on names so far until Akanksha came. All your names also might have been kept with a purpose like my own name had been. Shall we talk about it?" said Surya and continued, "We will start with Swetha."

"No, I won't be the first one. Let Imran start the discussion. Anyhow, he isn't eating anything now," said Swetha.

"No way, girls or Surya first," said Imran.

"I have a lot to tell and so will be the last one to say. Swetha will start now," said Surya.

"Okay," said Swetha and continued, "Well, Swetha means white or pureness. My dad likes the word very much and wanted me to be pure like my name. Being the only one left for him, I will be in his mind all the time and when he remembers me, all his negative intentions, if any, die down, as he puts it. This is what I know and that's the reason why he kept my name as Swetha. I will interview him for more details and update you with my findings," said Swetha.

"Okay dear, we accept what you said. Only you are pure and so is only your name. Everyone else here is impure and I am the superlative degree for the impure," said Surya.

"Idiot, it is you who asked me to tell the meaning of the name and when I tell the same, you make fun of me," said Swetha staring at the ground like a child does when it doesn't get what it wants.

Surya smiled at Swetha's response and looking at Siddharth said, "Now, it's Siddharth's turn."

"My father worked very hard neglecting even his health and earned lots of money. He craved for status and fame. He provided his mother all that she required, a house in the centre of the city and the servants to look after her. She seemed to be happy for what all her son had provided her. One day, when my dad was away for work, he received a telegram that revealed his mother's death. It was sudden, unexpected and he burst into tears. The doctor told that all through the years, she was alone worrying, yearning for something. Later on, through the servants, he came to know her wish for staying with his son and grandsons and not in this artificial happiness of the richness, but couldn't convey it to him as she thought that it might clash with his own interests. He lost his loving mother. He remembered the years she brought him up. All the money he earned seemed meaningless for him. With that money, he established an Ashram for the old where he spent a year peacefully. He searched for the meaning of life, studied all the classics, epics and tried to understand all the religions. It is there that he met my mother who was into social work and both of them married. When I was born, he did not want me to be after the meaningless life he had lived and so he named me as Siddharth, the original name of Gautama Buddha, his inspirer for life," said Siddharth his face completely calm while narrating the entire story.

"That's quite a story man. I didn't know it earlier. It is strange that we still have things to know though we have been together for a long time. The story behind the name is quite interesting, isn't it? Coming to the topic again, both of you are 'you' because of your respective fathers. Let me tell you about me. I am 'Surya' because of my mother. When I was in my stomach, sorry, my mother's stomach, she saw super star Rajnikanth's film Dalapathi. Rajnikanth's name in that film is Surya. As your fathers had their respective influences, my mother had an influence of Rajnikanth's character and instantly decided that the child's name would be Surya if it was a boy."

"That's quite a story man!" exclaimed everyone.

"That's only half the story. Did you forget my full name Surya Narayana Choudhary?"

"Teri maaki, then it is not even half the story. It's just one third," said Imran.

"Okay, one third as you said. Listen to the remaining two third. It's quite interesting and you will know more about India. I too was thrilled when I came to know about it for the first time."

"What else can we do? Continue it," everyone responded in a chorus.

"My mom told her Akanksha i.e. desire," saying this, he turned towards Akanksha, raising his eyebrows with pride that he has used her name in his talk and said, "my mom told her desire of naming me as Surya. But as you know, my dad always had plans for me. This time too, he had plans even though I didn't enter the world then. The twist in the story is, the plans are not for me but for him. He wants to be out of the birth and death pain cycle."

"Birth and death pain cycle, Oh God!" exclaimed everyone.

"Yeah, it is about God, as you said," continued Surya, "according to Hinduism, there is a continuous chain of births and deaths that everyone has to go through. I don't know the exact number, but to put it simply, our form changes many times like we change our clothes, but here, it is in a larger time-scale. There is nothing like eternal death. 'For one who is born, death is certain, for one who dies, birth is certain,' said Krishna to Arjuna in the Bhagawad Gita, as Arjuna was not willing to kill his own family members in the battle. The next life will be based on your present karma. If you like swimming a lot and swim most of the time, there are high chances that you become a fish in the next life. If you want to romance always, you will be born as a pigeon since it rarely does other work. If you have various interests, you will take the form which has the mixed effects of all the karmas. If you work very hard, you become a donkey. This is the way it goes. In the next life, as far as my prediction goes, Akanksha becomes a shopping mall owner. If you are like Imran, you will be born as a buffalo," and as Imran started hitting him, he moved aside and said, "Buffalo, since buffalo always keeps eating something. Like this, you have to take some lakhs of births, birth after death and death after birth. One important thing one needs to keep in mind is that human life is obtained because of the noble deeds in the previous life and is the only chance to get out of this birth and death cycle."

"All this is a suffering, according to my dad and to get out of this chain of birth and death, there is only one remedy. Apart from Karma, the thing that is there in your mind during the last moment of your death is also very important. If you remember God, you will go to God and if you remember work, you will become a donkey. Now my father is aiming to get out of this chain and he wants to use me in the process. You might have seen in the old movies when the parent is about to die, he wants to see his son or daughter and, so, calls their name. In the same way, my father, when he is about to die, intends to call my name Narayana as Narayana is the name of God. In turn, God Narayana would think that he is calling Him, break his birth-death chain and take my dad with Him. This is my dad's plan. For me to break the chain, I have to name my children after Gods or Goddesses. Had there been just one God, there might have been a confusion. So we have around 300 million Gods. That's why almost all the Indian names are Gods' names. Some of our elders go to the Himalayas and say Krishna or Rama for practicing this when they are about to die and thus break the chain. My grandmother is sure to break the chain since for every step she walks, she utters the word Krishna."

"That's quite a story man," exclaimed everyone.

"Now I understood why your father calls you as Narayana, but your mother as Surya," said Swetha lifting her eyebrows proudly.

Imran said, "Teri maaki, tell me again that I become a buffalo."

Swetha interrupted and said, "Imran, you need not worry. You are a Muslim and so this theory is not applicable for you."

"Even Swetha started joking," said Surya and as Swetha came to hit him, he moved aside and said, "Now comes the third part of my name, Choudhary."

Everyone uttered in unison, "We know about it. In fact, entire India knows. Even then, if you feel like telling it, tell it personally to Akanksha."

"Okay, on popular demand, I conclude here and pass on to Imran, the next-life buffalo" said Surya.

Now it was Imran's turn. He didn't know why his name was Imran. He thought about it for a while, "Just a minute," he said and continued, "You will hear it for the first time with me." He took his mobile, called his mother, switching on the speaker and said "Hello maa, why is my name Imran?"

"You dog, buffalo, donkey, idiot. Where have you been since morning? You haven't eaten anything. I prepared biryani for you and by the time I came out of the kitchen , you disappeared. Come home again, I will break your head, teri maaki," he switched off the mobile while his mother was still continuing with her blessings.

"I have said only buffalo. As a bonus, you also got dog, donkey and idiot from your mother," said Surya.

"Teri maaki..." Imran told as everyone started laughing even more.

Akanksha interrupted and said, "What is this teri maaki," that Imran keeps on using.

Swetha exploded laughing for this question and said, "Even this has got a wonderful history. Now it's the Hyderabadi history. Want to know it?"

"Yeah, surely," said Akanksha in excitement.

"Well, Imran's father used to look after this cafe when he was alive. Imran had to help his dad. Then he was a child and used to serve customers. The most frequent clause he heard was 'Teri maaki kir kiri'. He didn't know what they meant. He could understand all the other words except that. As he grew up, he heard it many times and every time he heard it, his curiosity to know the meaning of this mysterious word increased. One day when his curiosity reached its peak, he asked one of the regular customer Ismail Bhai, the one sitting there watching television, from whom he listened it the most. As far as I know, the conversation went this way.

Imran: Uncle, what is this so-called teri maaki kir kiri which you frequently use.

Ismail Bhai: You have asked a very good question, beta. I am glad that the question came from a child like you. I will tell you everything about it. Telling teri maaki kir kiri is one way of venting out our frustration. It gives a great relief the moment you utter it. As you know in India, many people from different regions speak Hindi. The way Hindi is spoken is different in all the Hindi-speaking areas. Every region has its own way of getting rid of frustration. Teri Maaki kir kiri is our way of getting rid of frustration.

Teri maaki kir kiri is not a recent clause, beta. It is the most famous clause in the whole world. It is an age-old interaction between different people from different countries that has formed it. It started as something else, crossed all the great lands like Iraq, Iran and Turkey, embracing the style and slang there, came here, reacted with our own language and has finally taken this shape. It was inherited by us long time back. Preserving it is now in our hands. One day, I was in England and you might have known that the British had ruled us. During their rule, we used this clause maaki kir kiri out of our frustration and they, in turn, used it to remove their own frustration caused by us, though the way they pronounced it was different. Nevertheless, it served the purpose. Those were the days of conversations. In one of my conversations in England recently, I uttered teri maaki. Then, the people there immediately realized that I am an Indian. After sometime, I uttered teri maaki kir kiri and they have realized that I am a Hyderabadi and received me warmly. We had discussions about the Nizam and our Charminar. To say in a single word, it is the sentence which makes you a Hyderabadi," said Swetha in the most dramatic way, trying to imitate Imran and Ismail Bhai as much as she could, adding value to the story that has already been told many times in the same café.

"Since then, Imran used the word as much as he can and uttered it wherever it was possible. His mother, in an attempt to make her son stop from uttering the word, quarreled with him for nearly six years and finally was able to remove the word kir kiri and so now, he uses only teri maaki. In her attempt to make her son stop from uttering this clause, she too learnt it and when very frustrated, she too uses this word, as you might have heard in her conversation with Imran," said Surya.

"That's quite a history, man," said Akanksha, for which everyone laughed.

"Guys, I really had a very good time. In fact, I've had some of the best moments of my life. It's really lovely hanging out with friends and sharing fun. I really had a great time and I am pretty sure, I can never forget your names. I too will tell you guys the reason for my name the moment I get to know about it from my parents," said Akanksha looking into Siddharth's eyes.

CHAPTER

3

Clash of Ideas

Akanksha left the scene. The orders of biryani increased, now that the sun moved down embracing the earth. India won the match as a result of which the biryani orders surged further. Everywhere, there were discussions about the match and Sachin's name was all around in the air. Crackers were being fired on the roads. People hugged each other as replays were continuously being telecasted.

"Sachin, Sachin, Sachin. This is the only word being uttered everywhere. This cricket God, with his mesmerizing style, is making the cricket-mad nation go crazy. I can't imagine the day he retires," said Surya.

"That will certainly be one of the saddest days in our cricket's history," said Swetha.

Siddharth, who was listening to the conversation, slowly raised his voice and said "Guys! I have decided to leave my job. I said the same to Swetha yesterday."

"Are you serious? What happened to you all of a sudden?" asked Surya.

"It is the same reason I have been telling you before. I am not able to digest the fact that I could eat and live comfortably while half the nation is starving. Every gulp of food I take, I feel as if I am taking it at the expense of other people."

"What has that got to do with your job? Will the half nation get food to eat, if you leave your job? Don't be foolish, Siddharth. I know that you are not foolish, but don't be so idealistic."

"I am not being idealistic, Surya. I am just applying my mind. Just spare a few seconds and come out of this senseless so called civilized world and think practically. If you were not born to your parents but to someone else who are starving, what would you have become? It is the same 'you' but with fate less parents I am talking about. The fact is that 'Birth' determines the fate of a child in India. It's just damn birth. The richest person in India or, in fact, in the entire world, they say and the media showers all kind of praises for what he has achieved. Compared to who is he rich? With whom has he participated? Did he participate with the child that is serving the tea there or the beggar who is lying on the pavement? Survival of the fittest, they say. Who are the participants? Who is actually in the game? It is just a game in which very few, in fact very, very few participate, acquire wealth and say that they have won the race. How are the superlative degrees such as richest, greatest and poorest justified when everyone has got a different beginning."

"Siddharth, what you said is right. I wouldn't have been the same if I weren't born to the same parents. I would have been in the streets begging if born to beggars or, in fact, have starved to death. I would have been a big industrialist or a politician if my parents were big industrialists or politicians. But the world is like this. It was like this in the past and will be so in the future. You always tell us about the great French and Russian revolutions. In spite of all the great revolutions, the fate of the poor didn't change. The theories about the Revolutions get neatly printed in the History books but the poor remain poor. History is the witness. In this modern era of disguised democracy, it is still impossible. For the people, of the people and by the people, they say, but as everyone knows, it is for the rich, of the rich and by the rich.

Parties need fund. The rich provide the fund and policies should favor them. This is how it is and it goes. But everything happens in the form of disguised promises and statements favoring the poor. Strangely, democracy is to consider the interests of all groups of society and how can all the interests be met when they clash? Take any group, be it minority or majority, religious or region, you find in it a group of rich exploiting the poor. It all has to happen this way, Siddharth. There is nothing we can do. Life has to proceed as it comes."

"How can you talk this way in spite of knowing the facts? Don't you have some moral responsibility? Don't you have some consideration for your fellow beings?" asked Siddharth.

"What can I do even if I have some consideration? I am helpless. Even if by some wonder, if you achieve what Marx has written and Lenin has dreamt, nothing is going to change. Say, by some wonder, if you have redistributed all the wealth and land of the rich among everyone equally and say if the economic equality is achieved, what happens next? Is there any guarantee that the classless society remains the same? Won't there be any more divisions of the rich and the poor?

Let's take a very simple and practical case. Say if there are two girls. One is beautiful while the other is not. Both are distributed wealth on par with the men in that society. After sometime, see how the income is likely to be redistributed. There are high chances that natural forces benefit the beautiful one. Siddharth, there are different types of people. All the greediness, oppression, exploitation, crookedness, kindness whatever it may be act on the society and finally it will be the same way as we are now today. See any country, developed or under developed, capitalist or communist, all these reactions happen.

You talked about everyone participating in the game. Let me tell you about my village. There, the village politician is crooked as in most other places. He is afraid that if the village children are educated, he might not get the votes. On the other hand, in the case of illiterates, some liquor or a biryani fetches him all the votes. So he makes sure that the school doesn't run properly. He manages the inspector by giving him some bribe. The point I want to convey is, for him to survive, people should not be educated. If people are educated, he can't survive. It is the clash of interests where, finally, the rich and the powerful win. Siddharth, I know I am not as intelligent as you but I am just trying to be pragmatic."

"It's heartening that you have mentioned about the great revolutions of the world. But the way your conclusions are derived are not true. It is true that even after the great revolutions, there still exists the rich and the poor. But earlier the wealth was in the hands of one or two. Now it is not. A vast thinking middle class has emerged which is now aiming big. Thoughts have developed and freedom has increased.

Our mothers and sisters... if they are able to move on the streets, if they are able to vote, they are doing it only because of the fact that they are the by-products of these revolutions. There were many changes that happened. The fact that you and I are able to debate about the fate of a country is a result of all these changes. Without us realizing, they have made me and you. At the same time, a major class is unaware of all these changes and opportunities and hence is exploited. I am not arguing for the land to be redistributed or rich to be made poor. That is inevitable and is surely going to happen someday. The only thing I am stressing is that they need an opportunity to participate in the race. For that everyone should be provided some basic things to start with.

These are the days when a girl walks on a ramp and boy exposes his muscles and earn lakhs and lakhs. There are many beautiful boys and girls who don't even know the way the world is or even if they knew, they are frightened or the social barriers stop. The moment they stop fearing, the moment they cross their barriers, the moment they know the world the way it is, the world of the rich is sure to crumble down. All we need is to give a push.

The way people can earn income is strange. But there

is no other alternative and we have to do it. Why should we all do this? Is there a need to do this?

We should do it because nothing is in our hands. Everything has to move according to the dictates of the big players of the world. We are just a paper that flies in the wind blown by them. World peace and solution to the problems is in the hands of those big players. With their will, everything desired by the humanity can be achieved. Suffering can be minimized and poverty can be eliminated. In spite of the two world wars due to the capitalistic aims which have almost destroyed the world, they have chosen this capitalistic path of survival of the fittest because they are the 'most fit ones' at present. They have invented beautiful words like efficiency, competition which convinces each and every soul and, in turn, makes the exploiter feel proud of this organized and ambitious world. Let them do all this. They should remember that this can't continue for long and can happen only till the exploited is ready to be exploited. The moment he begins to participate in it, the moment he knows the hidden meaning of the words they utter, it is the time for the big players to sweat and there are already visible signs of this change.

The rich are only rich till the poor are ignorant. The moment the poor realizes, the pillars of the rich tumble down and when they fall down, they have to learn living on the ground. This applies everywhere, be it a village or a town or a country or the entire world. Nobody is bound to be the rich forever. When everyone is ready to participate in the game, the inevitable happens. The wealth gets redistributed, lands get redistributed and the democracy becomes people's democracy. The same village politician will be forced to do good for the school. The only thing required is to ensure that everybody participate in the game. For a country like ours, it is the most vital thing. I am sure that the change is bound to come but I wanted to see the change as soon as possible and want to be a part of this change.

As you said, your village politician is interested in keeping those people illiterate. So go and establish the school and educate them. Don't you have the responsibility? Remember the tax money with which you have studied. Whose money is it?

You know, Surya, each time I take rice, I feel I am eating it at the expense of others. I don't know how the rich is digesting their food but I cannot. I want to be out of this selfish, purposeless life.

You and I are able to do anything because of some basic resources we have got. Everyone should be given that. Else, it is a crime in which we all are participating. Being a bit fortunate, it is our duty to educate them, enlighten them, show them the way, show them their strengths and their weaknesses."

Swetha interrupted and said, "Yes, Surya, I can earn few thousands and Siddharth a few more. We both like each other and, so, we can marry, live happily, have children, provide them good education, have some good savings for them in the form of land, house and money and ultimately die. They will, in turn, grow up and continue this same cycle. What have we done in the process? Is it the human life or a routine job like that of a robot? Is it a meaningful life or a few years in a parrot's cage? We just think it to be life but it is not so. It is much more meaningful if you reach the poor, care for them and visualize your family in them. People starving to death and dogs feeding on branded food cannot coexist. No civilized world should accept this."

"Teri maaki! Today you have debated the most. Siddharth, I support you and know that whatever you do, you do it with a purpose. Even quitting this job I guess might have been in your mind since long time. Surya wants to come with you but he is worried that if you go to some forest, he won't get any girl there to flirt with and so he is trying to change your minds. The day he gets frustrated with girls, he will join you for sure. All his philosophy about practicality is just for the practical reasons to flirt with girls."

"See who is lecturing on the philosophy of life? In villages, there won't be any biryani to eat... Let me see how you will join Siddharth if he leaves for the village," said Surya.

There were smiles all over again. "Surya, It's already late. I have to address the meeting and Imran will accompany me. You accompany Swetha to her house."

Swetha and Surya fared good bye to the others. Surya turned towards Siddharth and said, "Siddharth, whatever you say, I don't feel it is wise to quit the job. While doing the job, try to do some social service."

Siddharth smiled for what his friend suggested him and told, "Surya, observe the beggar on the pavement without clothes. What do you think is the difference between him and the model in the underwear ads?"

"Live as you wish and try to change the world. I prefer to live the way I receive the life. But remember, there comes a day when you realize that you are used by the people, left behind, feel lonely and realize what life is going to teach you," said Surya.

Siddharth smiled when Swetha interrupted and said, "One hour walk with Surya! I think I will be dead before I reach my home."

4

Good Friends

"So darling, shall we go?" said Surya with a mocking expression of closing his eyes and sticking his tongue out simultaneously.

"If you imitate me again, I will kill you then and there," said Swetha.

"Okay, sweet heart, you can kill me," said Surya once again repeating the expression.

"Enough is enough. Chalo, let's go," said Swetha with a smile.

"Swetha, it's long time since we walked together."

"Yeah, it's long time since someone happened to eat my brain."

Surya smiled at her reply and asked, "Can I ask you something?"

"I know that there is stock of questions eagerly waiting to come out of your brain. You can proceed."

"Why do most of the Guntur girls not reveal their mobile numbers?"

"Guntur girls! Oh God! Surya, I know you since my childhood. Can't you ask her number directly?" said Swetha.

"I know, Swetha. You are so intelligent. If you had tried, you would have become a CBI officer."

"Stop the flattery and listen. As far as I know, I don't have any friend from Guntur."

"Please tell me dear. If you don't help me, who else will?"

"I really don't have any friend from Guntur. Tell me the name of the girl, whose number you want," said Swetha.

"It is Sandhya."

"Sandhya is not from Guntur."

"It doesn't matter, Swetha. What really matters is her number which you know," said Surya and continued, "give me her number, dear. I promise you a panipuri treat."

"You are really an idiot, Surya. Last week, you took the number of Saroja and this week it's the turn of Sandhya. You really don't have any shame," said Swetha.

"Scold me as much as you can, Swetha. Everytime you scold, I feel as if some angels are showering heavenly blessings from the skies on me."

"You are really an idiot, Surya," said Swetha and continued "her parents are looking for a suitable match for her and so you have to forget her."

"It doesn't matter, Swetha. It's still in the initial stage, right? Moreover, I have come to know that she wants to date as early as possible since she is going be married soon."

"Who told you all this nonsense?"

"Imran researched it for me."

"You have taken the help of Imran as if there is no one else left for you to research about her. That fellow is unable to take the matter in case of Nasreen to the next stage and he is the one who is helping you. See how strange life is. By the way, what are the latest updates in their love story? Has it moved any further?"

"I am trying to do whatever I can to bring them together. But this useless fellow is spoiling everything. You know how difficult it is to bring her out. I did it with a lot of effort and you should have known what he asked her."

"What did he ask her?"

"Better to hear it from him," said Surya and took his mobile out to call Imran.

"Bol sale, what's the matter?" said Imran.

"Hello, Imran."

"Oh, Swetha, tell me. What's the matter?"

"Tell me what you told Nasreen when you met her last time."

"Me? I didn't tell her anything. I just told her that I was fine and enquired her how she was."

Swetha looked at Surya and shook her head to ask him the next step she is supposed to do.

"Ask him what he said just before that," whispered Surya.

"Even before that, what did you tell her?"Said Swetha

Imran thought about it for a while and said, "Last week, she prepared biryani and sent it to me. I told her that biryani was very good. What's wrong with that? Don't believe all that Surya tells you. He doesn't understand true love."

As Swetha began laughing, Surya took the mobile and said, "That's okay, Romeo. We have got what we wanted," and disconnected the call.

"You know how difficult it is to bring her out. With much difficulty, I brought her out and this fellow, as if there is nothing else to talk, talks about the biryani's taste. They had only 10 minutes to talk and there was complete silence for about eight minutes. Both of them looked into each other's eyes for a while and suddenly looked at the ground. It was a repeat telecast of about 10 times. She was a lot better than our hero and tried to talk something without fear. This fellow doesn't open his mouth throughout the conversation and when asked for the reason, tells me, "It's very difficult, yaar. In case of true love, whatever you think is really difficult. You just don't understand it."

After she leaves, he asks me in a low voice, "I want to talk to her again, Surya," as if he talked to her continuously and those 10 minutes were not enough for their speechless talk. Every day, he goes around her house about 10-15 times like a bill collector. As soon as she comes out, he hides. Nobody knows why the hell he goes there. Even our heroine is special in her own way. She realizes that her Romeo has come and so comes out to dry her towel around 10-15 times. What a great love story to watch, you know!"

Swetha burst out in laughter and said, "It's not going to happen with you around. I should take the matter into my hands and see that they come closer."

"Ok, leave Nasreen for a moment and tell me about Sandhya."

"I told you that her parents are looking matches for her. If I hear her name again from you, I am going to kill you right at this moment."

"Okay dear, don't be so angry. Let's forget about Sandhya. Do you know one thing, Swetha? I have always wondered how you turned out to be such a great and mature person. The moment I came to know you were born on 25th October i.e., the day the Russian Revolution began, everything became clear to me. Really, birthdays do matter a lot, right?"

"Stop the flattery and tell me whose birthday you want to know?"

"I know, Swetha. You are so intelligent. If you had tried, you would have become a CBI officer."

"Surya, stop the flattery. You might have forgotten, but I didn't. You have used the Russian revolution idea six times before to know the birthdays of six of my friends."

"Please tell me the details of your friend with whom you were talking at the Ameerpet bus stand."

Swetha thought for a while and said, "Ameerpet bus stand! Just a second. Let me think, Ameerpet bus stand... Yesterday... "

"The one in the blue jeans," said Surya.

"Yeah! the one in blue jeans, right? She is not my friend. She's my junior..."

"Do you know her name, place, birthday, mobile number, tastes, etc."

"Etc! Will there be anything more than the data you have asked for? You are really an idiot, Surya."

"Okay, I agree that I am an idiot but please tell me her details, Swetha."

"Before I tell her details, I want to know the reason for your break-up with Saroja. Everything was fine between you guys. It was just the last weekend you both met on the Necklace Road where you composed a poem describing how important she was to you than Lord Buddha. The same day she called me and told that she loves you so much and thanked me for introducing you to her. Yesterday, she called me again and cried telling that everything was over between you both. What happened all of a sudden?"

"Yes, she was wonderful and different from most of your friends. She recharged my mobile and paid the bill wherever we went. Sometimes, she paid Imran's bill too. She woke me up early in the morning with her morning call and she remembered my entire schedule."

"She remembered your schedule as if you had a very busy schedule," Swetha interrupted.

"Eating panipuri is also an important part of a schedule in love. All Siddharth and you know, is exploiters, exploited and the society. There is lot to experience in love. Sometime, you guys better take a leave from all your routine things and try to love. Then the things I am impressing upon might make some sense to you. I think I am deviating from the break-up story. Now don't interrupt me till I end it. She used to call me around 20 times a day. Everyday used to end with her good night message and the next morning she used to tell me about the dreams she had about me. Sometimes, I told my dreams too. Then I thought, the time for us to meet had arrived. Everything turned out well in the meeting. The fact that I gave her more importance than Lord Buddha almost brought tears from her eyes. After that, we strolled on the Necklace Road where I repeated that I would give up the entire world for her. She felt happy and said that she loved me so much. Everything was going smooth like the Rajdhani Express, but as you know, even the Rajdhani has got its own problems. Suddenly, I came across the poster of Katrina Kaif and, as usual, she was very hot. For a moment, I forgot the world around me and stared at her till the sounds of the traffic brought me to the real world. From the next moment, she's changed."

"What happened?"asked Swetha.

"She walked towards me angrily and said, 'Why do you lie to me? I hate you' and then started moving away from me. I asked her what the lie was. She repeated the dialogues which I uttered a few minutes before when I told her that I would forgo the entire world for her. She told me that I forgot her just for the sake of Katrina Kaif poster. Don't I have the right to stare at the poster of Katrina Kaif? She is so possessive, Swetha. I tried to convince her and told her that she too can look at the poster of Salman Khan when I was beside her and I had no problem with that. But my idea did not convince her. Today, she messaged me and said, 'if it's the case only with celebrities, it doesn't matter.' But I didn't want to be with her any more. Of course, all the recharges and bills have to be paid by me now, but I have peace of mind. I feel like I have attained Nirvana like Lord Buddha. Someday, if I get your call when I am with her, she might ask me to stop talking to you. Just tell me, for her sake, how can I stop talking to you? Is she more important to me than you?" asked Surya.

"Should I believe this? Is it just for this reason that she broke up with you?" asked Swetha.

"Of course, Swetha. It is for this reason."

"I don't think so. Saroja is not a fool," said Swetha.

"Okay, let me tell you the exact story. It was not Katrina Kaif, but a very beautiful girl like you who was walking beside us. As she was looking too good, I looked at her and Saroja didn't like it. The remaining part is exactly what I have said before. You have to believe it, Swetha. I promise on the girl whose details you are going to tell me."

"Oh God, once again the girl. Ayyo, you are really an idiot, Surya. I am not going to give you the details of any girl. What you have done is enough."

"Please tell me dear. If you don't help me, who else will?"

"Okay, she is Sushmitha, my junior. She got around

five proposals till now and has rejected all of them. I don't have her contact number and you will have to grease my palms for that. "

"I know that you'll definitely help in finding me a suitable match. I promise that this will be the final number you will be giving me."

"If you would have committed yourself to a single girl, I, definitely, would have helped you as much as I could. Everytime you ask me a new contact number, you promise me that it will be the last one."

"Don't we have a look at a lot of dresses before selecting the final one? This is the case of selecting a life partner, Swetha, and so we need to be even more careful. That is what I am trying to do."

"Okay baba, do as you wish. The moment I get her number, I will ask her and if she agrees, will give it to you. I don't want any bribe for that."

"Thank you very much, dear. I cannot imagine my love life without you."

*****

"Swetha, is that bus number visible to you?"

"Yeah, it is 1V. Can't you see it?"

"I forgot to tell you. I am unable to see things clearly. Day before yesterday, I went for an eye checkup and found that I have defect of vision. It is minus point five for my left eye and minus point one for my right eye. Why is the eye sight different when I open and close my eyes at the same time? I asked the doctor, but he had no answer."

"You might have always sat on the left of the girls in college," said Swetha.

"Was that supposed to be a joke?" said Surya

"Was your question supposed to be joke?"

"Okay, leave it and tell me why girls walk as if they are walking on some thorns? Is there something really wrong or is it they want to walk that way thinking it to be stylish?"

"Why do you pester me with your senseless questions, Surya?"

"Please answer me, Swetha."

"I don't know, you should have asked Saroja. She walks that way, right?" asked Swetha with a mocking expression of closing her eyes and sticking her tongue out simultaneously.

"Okay, tell me why they try to move their lips a little while talking. Can't they talk naturally?"

"Ask the girl who does that and why do you talk as if only girls do that. Tell me why boys talk more than what is necessary. Why do they move their lips more than what is necessary?"

"Siddharth does that right? I will tell that idiot not to repeat it again," said Surya.

"Idiot."

"I agree that I am an idiot, dear, but you tell me this. Everyone has got some plans about the way they should be married? What is your plan?"

"You should not make fun of me after I reveal it."

"Why would I do that, Swetha? You are my closest pal," said Surya.

"It's okay then. I should sit on a horse and Siddharth should come on an elephant. By seeing me, the elephant should raise its trunk to salute me with a garland and place me alongside Siddharth. Then we have to move on the streets on that elephant."

"Where should we sit Swetha? Do you have any plans for that? Elephant, horse, at least a goat?"

"This is not fair, Surya. You promised you will not tease me..."

"Sorry dear, continue the story."

"Those were all my childhood dreams and all my desires died down slowly. Now, I want my marriage to be very simple and don't want it to be the way people conduct it nowadays where the sole aim is to show their social status. It won't be in a closed room or in a temple or a church. It will be just like one of our meetings in the café. I want only my closest pals to attend it for whom my marriage brings utmost satisfaction. There shouldn't be any auspicious time or time limits. There should be real smiles everywhere. My friends should be visualizing my future then and there. Both of our desires we had earlier have to act and react with each other and take a common form there and should bind us. It should be the official merging of souls which were longing since long time to come together. Angels should be pleased to see my marriage and request my Lord to allow them to witness my marriage on earth."

"Shall I tell how your marriage will take place? Both of you will be in some remote village then. Siddharth will be with full beard like the sages in the puranas. You will be like the exhausted Sita during the exile. You will then be the mother of the forest. All your guests will be monkeys and snakes and all the wild animals. The marriage orchestra will be the croaking of the frogs."

And as Surya continued, Swetha interrupted him saying, "Everything is a joke for you. It's foolish on my part to tell you my plans."

Surya replied, "Sorry dear, don't be angry. Will I be there in your closest pals list for your marriage?"

"You won't be on my list. You might be there in Siddharth's list," said Swetha.

"Don't be angry, Swetha. We have almost reached your house. If your dad sees his little girl angry, he will chop me off into pieces. It's time for me to leave; else your father might catch me and preach what life is. Good night and bad dreams, dear."

CHAPTER

Universal Brotherhood

Siddharth rang the bell. Swetha, who was in the kitchen, came to open the door. She was wearing a plain blue sari.

"Hello, Swetha."

"Hi, Siddharth, how was the meeting yesterday?"

"It was fine. You look great in this sari."

"Is it?" said Swetha with a smile and added, "Where is Surya?"

"Surya had to accompany Akanksha for some shopping."

Swetha smiled and said, "After the shopping, he would definitely have a lot to tell about," and added, "Yesterday, all along the way, he pestered me with his questions. But his stupid questions are really fun to listen, right?"

"He likes to irritate you, Swetha. He never does that with anyone else."

While talking, they reached the hall where, Swetha's dad Ravindra was resting on a chair.

Swetha passed on the remote to Siddharth and went towards the kitchen.

"Namaste, Uncle," said Siddharth and sat beside him.

"Namaste, beta," said Ravindra, placing the book which he was reading on the table.

Ravindra is about 60 years old. He has a long beard and sharp and attractive eyes which he rarely blinks.

"How is everything going on, Siddharth?"

"Pretty well, uncle," said Siddharth.

"How is Swetha?"

"She is fine uncle."

"Yeah, she is fine. I find her very happy now and by seeing my little girl smiling most of the time, I feel very happy."

"She likes our company, uncle."

"I guess so and hope that it continues forever. What else do I require other than seeing her happy always? I don't know why but I feel like telling you something. When Swetha was born, the first time I took her in my hands, the happiness I got can never be defined in words. Tears rolled over my cheeks seeing my little girl. The day she opened her cute small eyes, I can never forget. . Since then, everything she did gave me utter joy. All were very small things but I found immense pleasure in them. The way she moved her little hands, the way she blinked her eyes, the way she caught my legs when I was about to move, I can never forget in my life. Those were the years of utmost satisfaction in my life. I realized that there can be nothing joyous than these.

Then I lost my wife. It was a sudden death and it came as a shock to me. All her memories haunted me. It was a very difficult phase of my life and I felt as if I had lost my world. It had an impact on Swetha too. Ever since she lost her mother, I was very much worried about her. She grew up lonely. She never made friends and as she grew up, she became bold. She was not like other girls and she hated this male-dominated society of ours. She wanted to be independent. As she lost her mother, I gave her complete freedom. In fact, I wanted her to be the way she wanted. But somewhere in my mind, there was always a feeling that it might lead her into trouble. Ever since you became close to her, she is changed. Surya, Imran and your company changed her. She was never so happy before. The moment she heard the bell ring, there was a glow in her face. I find her very happy nowadays. She talks as if she has found everything she wanted. There is satisfaction in her eyes. I could see the first day's glow in her eyes again. There is always a smile over my little girl's face. Now I think I can rest peacefully seeing you people together."

"Uncle, the changes in Swetha are visible. But the changes in me are not so. There were many changes in me since she entered my life. She has been the biggest moral force in me. She changed my world, my views, my goals and my outlook towards life. As an individual, I feel I have grown up so much after meeting her. All of a sudden, life has become meaningful to me. Without her and your qualities imbibed in her, this wouldn't have happened. I have become so dependent on her that I cannot do any task without having the presence of her mighty face. "

"It is good to hear all this from you. I knew that Christ would never leave me alone," said Ravindra.

"Uncle, I am planning to leave my job."

"Quit the job?"

"Yeah, I have been thinking about it for a while and I am almost convinced about it now. My father has no objection. But fear about Swetha's future is haunting me."

"What is your plan then?" asked Ravindra.

"These inequalities in the distribution of wealth keep haunting me. The sight of people begging on the streets is making me feel ashamed. I want to go to some less fortunate villages to do some meaningful service there."

"Does Swetha know this?"

"Yes, she knows."

"Well, as Swetha's father, this idea should not appeal to me. But I would be selfish if I hold back your good thoughts. I appreciate your thought, but talk to Swetha about it and both of you arrive at a decision regarding your future course of action. "

"Yeah, I will definitely do that," said Siddharth.

"Since you have told me about social service to the needy, I want to tell you something which might be of some help to you. When everyone was sending their children to the States to study more income-generating courses like Engineering and Law, Tagore sent his son to study Agriculture. Maybe our country and its poor villages were in the great poet's mind. He could have lived a very comfortable life in air-conditioned rooms, but he preferred to settle down in Shantiniketan, experimenting in studies and educating the poor. Remember that great person always. He might give you enough moral force in case of any doubt. All one needs, at present, is just to stop for a while in this busy strange world and think what he/she is doing. The real problem is that they are not having enough time to stop and think.

World is strange for we are strange
What we really want and what we are after
  We think are the same but are different
Eyes glow as the heart glows
May be this is the reason, we don't see our eyes
For if we see that glow, we know what we want
World is strange for we are strange

One thing you need to bear in mind, Siddharth. Education is a recent development. It is not the final answer to everything. It has got its advantages along with the disadvantages. In the olden days, when there was no formal education, the exploitation prevailed. These days, where the dowry increases exponentially with the degrees of the bridegroom, education has got no social role. All these inequality and oppression don't end even if everyone is educated. Being educated or making them educated is only the process of making them understand that they are being exploited and making them ready to fight against the exploiters. In our country, where a large chunk of population doesn't know what is happening in the world, educating them is the most important thing to be achieved. They need to know how other people are earning and how the rich and the poor co-exist. The more it gets delayed, the bigger the crime we are committing. The moment they are educated, they are sure to question the existing system. By education, we are providing an equal platform for everyone and this is the most basic thing to be provided. The potential of the education system is to alter the existing system or, at least, to change it to some extent. But we have to bear in mind that there is again the possibility of oppression from the new fortunate group to the other group in a civilized manner. The oppression never ends. Universal brotherhood is not an easy thing to achieve. Achieving universal brotherhood was, is and will be the biggest question since ages and is limited only to the theory.

Plato was frustrated with the way wealth was distributed as far back as the fifth century BC. In his quest to find answers for this, he came up with a beautiful theory. According to him, the institution of marriage should be abandoned. The matter of love should be left to the individual. Anybody can mate with anyone and the moment a child is born, he is to be taken away from the parents to be kept in a State nursery. The State has to take care of all the children, provide all the basic amenities and then after they reach a certain age, a few processes of elimination take place to allot them their respective social roles. The most essential thing is that the parents shouldn't know the child and the child shouldn't know the parents.

How harsh this theory sounds to the modern world? But if you see through what was going on in Plato's mind, you see how frustrated he was with the mankind and their efforts to make their children prosperous. Modern world does the same thing. To provide our children with the wealth and make them settle in good jobs, we do everything possible. The fact that we have our own children makes us least bothered about other children and this is the root cause for all inequalities and oppression. So, Plato had to use such harsh ideas.

This theory doesn't seem to be practically achievable but we can understand the basic cause of suffering. If children are not to be given to the State, the only alternative is to treat everybody like our own children. There is no other alternative.

Alexander was really great because of the things his father had provided him. The education, the planning, the well-trained army and the perfect mentor guide he had got made him Alexander the Great. If his father hadn't provided these, there are high chances that Alexander might not have been so great. Akbar was great because of what his ancestors had left behind. Now in our poor villages, many little Alexanders and Akbars are waiting for their mentors for guidance. Lack of guidance is driving these young ones to the fields. It is our duty to show them the way.

If I don't encourage you because of the fact that you will be marrying my daughter, I would be the most selfish person on the earth and all the knowledge of the books that I have gained by reading and teaching would be useless. With my whole heart, I wish you good luck, my boy. Just have faith in what you choose to do and proceed. Christ always stressed the word 'faith' more than anything else for it is with which you can achieve anything. Have faith in God and the work that you do. May Lord's blessings be with you all the time. "

Swetha returned from the kitchen and looking at both of them deeply immersed in their discussions said, "Only God can bring you guys back to this world when you are into some discussion. Both of you again lie to me that I am the most important one in your lives. When the discussion to change the world comes, you forget your so-called sweet world."

Ravindra and Siddharth smiled at their loved one's response. The three of them had the softdrinks that Swetha had prepared. Siddharth and Swetha then went out for a walk.

*****

"Today, you look very beautiful, Swetha."
"Oh, is it?"
"How do I look?"
"I don't know."
"You don't know?"
"Yeah, I don't know."
"Okay, what is your plan today?"
"I don't know."
"You don't know?"
"Yeah, I don't know."

"What happened to you, Swetha?"

"Nothing."

"Did I do something wrong?"

"No."

"Won't you speak to me?"

"No."

"What should I do to make you speak?"

"Nothing like that, I am okay."

"Swetha, see how beautiful that bird is!" Siddharth was pointing at a bird which was sitting on a tree.

"Yes, it is beautiful. If we could hear it sing, it would be even more beautiful," said Swetha, looking at the bird.

"Let's see for some time, hopefully, it might sing for you."

"It never sings here, Siddharth. It might have forgotten to sing. Singing automatically comes from within, the moment they find everything in sync with them. The process would initiate automatically when fresh air passes them and their hearts get tuned to the flow of the rivers in the flowering springs. It couldn't feel the same here and is left with no option other than to somehow feed her little stomach."

"Where does it find everything in sync with itself?"

Swetha didn't speak as the words couldn't come out, turned towards the other end and said in a trembling voice, "In a village with its loved one, Siddharth."

"Look into my eyes and speak."

Swetha remained silent and so Siddharth turned towards her, moved his hand to catch her chin, slowly raising it and then looking straight into her eyes said, "What happened Swetha? Won't you tell me?"

"I heard you and dad speak."

"Oh, I got the reason now. I am sorry if I have hurt you but this is a serious issue. I have been worrying about your future as a result of my decision. You would be very happy and can lead a comfortable life in case you decide to stay here. Otherwise, it would be a tough life and so I want you to think carefully before proceeding further. My heart always craves for you. But it is my duty to know your wishes and desires. Your father also advised me the same."

"Of course, I will accompany you, Siddharth, and I will be very happy to do that. How can I stay away from you? What is more satisfactory to me than staying with you and sharing all the hurdles you face, along with the happiness?"

"I know it, Swetha. But it is not that simple. I want you to take some time and think about it."

"I think you better know the heart of that bird, Siddharth. Nothing else is important to it than being with its loved one."

Siddharth held Swetha's face and looking deep in to her eyes said: "I know that you would never leave me, Swetha."

"I know you can't leave me, Siddharth," said Swetha with a smile, wiping the tears that were just coming out.

"How much time shall we be there? Shall we stay there till we die?" asked Siddharth.

"Yeah, we shall take our parents there. Later on, Surya and Imran will accompany us."

"Will they join us?"

"One day, they will definitely join us."

"Where shall we marry? Here or there?"

"Marriage in the village, doesn't it sound interesting?" asked Swetha.

"How many children shall we have? Is a dozen okay for you?"

"Dozen!" exclaimed Swetha and continued, "Then where do we have the time to do service?"

"Is three okay then?"

"You might keep their names as Plato, Socrates or Voltaire. Like my father and you have discussions, you and our children will have discussions leaving me alone."

"So what shall we do then? Shall we have no children?"

"I prefer not to have children..."

"Why? Is it because of what your father said about achieving universal brotherhood?"

"In a way, yes."

"But I want to see my little Swetha. I want to play with her and tell her all that you have done to me."

"Even I want to see little Siddharth. But we prefer not

to have. We have a big goal to achieve. There are many children waiting for us and we will go in search of them. We will not worry about the obstacles and will be together under any circumstances. We will sleep beneath a tree, live in a hut and eat what we get. Whatever the circumstances may be, we will be together without panicking about the future. "

"Your words give me strength, Swetha. But is it practically possible? What if we feel like seeing a film in a multiplex? What shall we do then?"

"We will look into each other's eyes."

"Yeah, your eyes Swetha, what beautiful eyes God has given you. Whenever I feel depressed, just come before me so that I can look into your eyes. You are my wealth, Swetha!"

"Are my eyes really that beautiful?"

"Ask the bird to look into your eyes and see its response."

"What would it do?"

"It would sing even if it doesn't have all those you have mentioned."

"You flatter me so much."

"I am just giving vent to my feelings. Maybe everyone feels the same about their loved one, I don't know… but I feel it."

"Yeah, me too. Do you know, I am using the eyelashes since you like it."

"I can notice the changes and I love them."

"I too love your eyes so much. The waves they send hypnotize me."

"There is one more beautiful thing than your eyes."

"Only one thing," said Swetha with a mocking expression of closing her eyes and sticking her tongue out simultaneously.

"I am not kidding, it's true."

"What is it?"

"Your smile, what a wonderful smile God has given you, Swetha? When I am about to die, just come and smile before me so that I can die happily with satisfaction."

"Don't talk like that, Siddharth."

"I really mean it, Swetha. I have no worries when you are with me."

"Me too."

"How can I repay God for giving you to me, Swetha?"

"Return to him along with me."

"I will definitely do that. But as an advance, smile once for God's sake, Swetha."

"No."

"Please, Swetha…"

"How can I smile without any reason?"

"Please, Swetha…"

"No."

"Please, Swetha…"

"No."

"Please Swetha…"

"You are an idiot, Siddharth," and before she could complete her sentence, Siddharth again said, "Please dear…"

"You are…" said Swetha with a smile that she couldn't control.

"Yeah, like this."

"Smile once again for my sake, Swetha."

"No."

"Please…"

"No."

The Shock

Siddharth, Swetha and Imran were sitting in the café which was not so crowded yet. Surya arrived along with Akanksha. His face looked pale as if he had lost everything in the world. Just outside the café, an old woman of about 80 with her bent back, was standing unable to cross the road. Imran noticed her and went towards her.

"Let me help you, Maaji," said Imran as the woman gave her hand.

"Thank you very much, my son, for rescuing this old one. The traffic has reached its peak. It is extremely difficult for me to cross the road."

"Why do you come alone to these busy places? Can't you come with someone? Don't you have anyone?"

The old woman smiled and said, "I have two sons and half a dozen grand children, beta. But everyone is extremely busy. They have left me long back to settle in the US. They say it is the land of riches and went away. I too don't want to disturb them from enjoying their comforts. Everyone is leaving nowadays and why didn't you leave your parents and go?"

"Not everyone is like your sons."

The old woman smiled like an enlightened soul after hearing what Imran had just said.

"Why are you smiling?"

"I have been hearing this since long time and so I laugh when I hear someone say it. I can tell you with most certainty that your time too will come one day."

"Whatever is the case, I will never leave my mother. I cannot convince you now."

"Don't be angry, my son. I am just telling you the way it happens."

"Anyhow, I am sorry about your children. I hope, one day they will surely come back looking for you."

"They never come, beta. They just tell me that they will come soon. The light of my candles leads me to darkness by looking for them but they never return."

"Then how do you earn your livelihood?"

"I used to have a shop but I sold it and deposited the money in the bank. I lost interest in business and money since my sons were sending me money thinking that all I need is money. I stopped receiving the money too and I survive on the interest that I get from the bank."

"So you feel very lonely, isn't it?"

"I got used to it, dear. I think about God most of the time and if there is any time left, I look at the photographs of my grandsons and granddaughters."

"Where is your house?"

"The one where the dog is sitting. That dog is the only companion I have got and her name is Tinku, my granddaughter's name. She is very understanding and never leaves me. It is good that dogs don't have education like us, else they might also be leaving for the US," said the old woman with a voice that indicated the depth of loneliness she was experiencing.

"Ok maaji, now we are through the road. "

"America is land of riches, right."

"Yeah, it is the richest country in the world."

"So everyone there will have a car, I guess."

"They have two or three cars. Even your son might have 3 cars."

"Then I guess the traffic there will be much more than here. How difficult it should be for my grandsons and granddaughters to cross the busy roads."

"Nothing happens to them, maaji. It is a well-planned country and so you need not worry about them," said Imran.

"I hope so, beta."

"It is very nice talking to you. One day, I will come and give you good company. Till then, take care of your health."

"God bless you, beta," said the old woman and headed towards her house as Tinku approached the old woman at the sight of her.

Imran was on his way back when a ball, which was hit by a child playing cricket, came towards him.

"Uncle, ball please," said the little one.

"Do I look like an uncle?"

"Bhayya, give me the ball."

"That's good," said Imran and threw the ball towards the little boy.

"Thanks, uncle," said the little boy in a funny way and ran as fast as he could.

Imran smiled at the boy and came back remembering his good old childhood days. He observed Surya who was sitting as if he had lost everything in the world. He looked at Siddharth and Swetha one after the other to know the reason without any outcome.

Swetha intervened and said, "Hello hero, what happened to you? Why are you so silent today?"

Surya didn't speak and remained silent.

"What happened to Surya, Akanksha? Why is he not speaking?"

Akanksha also remained silent.

Seeing everyone confused, Surya slowly raised his voice and said, "My marriage is fixed. The girl is my dad's friend's daughter. She belongs to my caste and is ready to give huge amount of money as dowry. I opposed, but nobody would listen to me as everything is already finalized. I don't know a damn detail about her but my marriage is fixed with her."

"Whoa! That's big news. Did you like her? Is she good-looking?" said Swetha.

"They gave me her photograph but I didn't see it. It

doesn't matter as things are not going to change with my tastes. Bloody caste and bloody dowry, that's all they need. They will marry me to a donkey if she is from my caste and huge dowry is offered. "

"You should have seen the picture, known her details, frankly told your opinion and then must have seen the consequences," said Imran.

"You know my father since childhood. It should happen the way he thinks. He tells me that I will surely come to know about the fruits of his deeds sometime later. He doesn't give a damn about my wishes. If I tell him that I want to marry Swetha, he will give a second thought about her too. There is no way people can convince him. Well, there is no point in arguing about it as things are already fixed. One good thing which might please you is that the girl is from a village and the marriage is fixed for the next month. It will take place in her village in coastal Andhra."

"After all, they are your parents and they know about you more than anyone else. She is your dad's friend's daughter and so your dad might have known her since a long time. Maybe she is the perfect one for you. Now that everything is fixed, just make up your mind for that and plan positively for the future. As for us, marriage in a village in coastal Andhra is a gift from your side," said Siddharth.

"Yeah, what Siddharth said is right. She might be a perfect match for you. Maybe she will be looking like Aishwarya Rai, who knows!" said Swetha.

"Aishwarya Rai! From a village! Please Swetha, I have already become a fun object and please don't make fun of me anymore."

"Now that Surya is going to be married, there will be no more dates, no more enquiries about my friends and I am definitely going to miss them in future. Poor Surya is going to be married and look at his face once, I want to see him in the canopy as soon as possible," said Swetha.

"You might have seen her picture, right? Tell us how she looks," said Swetha turning towards Akanksha.

"When the bridegroom itself is not interested, how

will I be? I also thought of seeing her during the marriage," said Akanksha.

"So all of us will be seeing her along with Surya during the marriage," said Swetha.

"That's a very good idea. What do you say, Surya?" said Imran.

"Please, let's talk about something else. I came here to get some relief."

*****

"Surya promised me to take to some good places in Hyderabad along with you guys but as soon as he heard his marriage news, he changed his mind. It's been a month since I came to Hyderabad and I haven't seen anything yet, not even the Charminar. Now that we have an occasion, I think this is the right time to go."

"What is the occasion?" asked Surya.

"What else? It's your marriage!" said Swetha.

"Please dear, let's go to Charminar. It could change Surya's mood," said Akanksha.

"I also haven't see the Charminar since a long time. I think it's a good idea. I need to buy some bangles for Surya's marriage," said Swetha.

"Let's book a cab then," said Akanksha.

"Cab! Don't you use public transport at all?" said Imran.

"I use it rarely."

"To experience any Indian city, the best way is to travel as a common man does rather than a tourist. Travelling in the city buses will give you better feel of the city than anything else. It gets you in direct touch with the common man and makes you understand the city better," said Siddharth.

Akanksha looked into Sidharth's eyes quite impressively and said, "I agree as our leader says."

All of them moved towards the bus stop and stood there waiting for the bus. A bus arrived which was completely packed with people, leaving no space for even air to pass through.

Akanksha, who was frightened just by looking at the condition of the bus, said, "I will avoid visiting Charminar than travelling in this bus. I will die out of breath if I get into this bus. God! How are people travelling in these horrible conditions? See the students on the footboards, 95 per cent of their body is outside the bus."

"Why are you so frightened, Akanksha? Haven't you travelled in a completely-packed bus any time? This is everyday routine here and we are accustomed to this kind of life style. Swetha travelled all her school and college days in these buses," said Surya.

"Swetha can get a Nobel Prize for all the patience she has got. As far as I am concerned, I am not going to travel in it at any cost," said Akanksha.

"Don't worry Akanksha, there are other provisions for people like us. We will wait for an Express or an air-conditioned bus," said Surya.

As soon as the Express bus arrived, all of them got in to it and Akanksha sat beside Surya.

"Lesson number one for you dear, observe the color of the seat on which Swetha is sitting. Those seats are reserved for women. It is better for you to sit there since this bus also gets crowded soon and you might again be irritated while getting down," said Surya.

Akanksha went and sat on the seat, yellow in color where it was indicated in Telugu that the seats were reserved for women.

Akanksha started to have the glimpses of the old city when Swetha pointed her finger out and said, "This is Mozamzahi market which Ismail Bhai keeps telling in his stories. It is a very old market and was built during the Nizam's time."

"Ticket! Ticket! There is a checking point soon. If there is someone left who has not taken the ticket, please take it, else you will be fined," said the conductor.

Akanksha took a 500-rupee note from her purse and said, "Five tickets to Charminar, please."

"Do you think I am the owner of the Reserve Bank of India? From where should I get the change for everyone? Can't you go in a separate cab if you have so much money?" said the conductor who was already irritated by seeing many big notes since morning.

"Sorry uncle, she has come from the US and she doesn't know the charges here. Those guys sitting behind us will take the tickets for us" said Swetha to the conductor pointing towards Surya and Siddharth.

"So you are going to see the Charminar and Mecca Masjid?" enquired the conductor with a smile.

"Yes," replied Akanksha.

"So you lived in the US since your childhood?" he asked.

"Yes," replied Akanksha.

"Will the US conductors have the same difficulties we have here? Will the buses be so crowded there?"

"The buses are never crowded there."

"Yeah, why will they be crowded? If they are so, they can buy a few more buses. They have got a lot of money, right. I have seen in movies, their roads are very good and so, the buses also will be in a good condition. My bus goes to the shed at least once in a month even if the most experienced driver is allotted. My neighbor's son says that in the US the bus movement can be tracked in a display. He went there to study and he sends about a lakh every month. It is the place where everyone earns so much, I guess. Won't there be any beggars there like we have them here in Hyderabad?"

As the questionnaire of the conductor continued, Surya intervened and said, "Five tickets to Charminar."

The conductor gave the tickets when a few students hurriedly got into the running bus and said, "Conductor sir, give two tickets to Dilsukhnagar."

The conductor again got irritated and said, "From where do all the people come to spoil my mood? Didn't you see the board while getting in? This bus doesn't go to Dilsukhnagar."

One of the students replied, "Sorry uncle, we didn't see the board."

"Will you marry a girl without seeing her? You will never do that, but you get into the bus without seeing the board. These young fellows are born just to kill me. They have time to observe every girl in the bus stop but have got no time to look at the boards," and then shouted, "Driver saab, stop the bus for two seconds."

The bus stopped and the conductor looking at the students said, "Chalo, get down and catch 225D or 156 to go to Dilsukhnagar."

As soon as the students got down Swetha said, "Conductor uncle, see this fellow, he is my friend Surya and he is marrying without seeing the bride."

"What happened to him, beta?"

"Fate uncle, fate!" replied Swetha.

"It doesn't matter, beta. You will get a very nice one. Even Sri Ramji was ready to marry Sita without having a look at her," said the conductor and left the scene to collect the tickets.

"Surya is going to get a bride like Sita Devi," said Swetha for which the conductor too smiled along with everyone.

The crowd in the bus increased. Swetha pointed her finger out and said to Akanksha, "This is the Afzalgunj Bridge where our hero met the heroine Bhagyamati for the first time. It was for her the Charminar was built and the city was named after her."

"Is this the reason why Hyderabad is called Bhagyanagar?" asked Akanksha.

"Yes, she has got another name too, Hydermahal and so the city is Hyderabad," replied Swetha.

"So, this is the city born out of love. That's quite interesting!"

"You will feel his love for her as soon as you see Charminar," said Swetha.

All the five of them got down from the bus with difficulty and began to walk.

"Why did we get down? Aren't we going to Charminar?" said Akanksha.

"Don't worry about Charminar, Akanksha. We are not going to return without showing you the Charminar," said Surya.

They were at the Afzalgunj Bridge and Akanksha asked, "This is the place where that guy proposed to the girl, right?"

"Who is the girl and who proposed to her?" asked Surya.

"The one for whom the Charminar is built," said Akanksha innocently, not aware of the fact that Surya had asked her sarcastically.

"Yeah, this is the same bridge," said Swetha.

"Shall we try the proposal scene? It will be very funny. The present hero and heroine, Siddharth and Swetha will perform it," said Imran.

"I am a very bad actor. I am not going to do it," said Siddharth.

"Surya will do it then. Now that he can no more date and propose to girls, let's give him a final chance," said Imran.

"In real life, anyway, Siddharth is going to be your hero. At least here, give me the chance to become your hero. I will make my last proposal memorable," said Surya, with a mocking expression of closing his eyes and sticking his tongue out simultaneously.

"Idiot, you imitated me so much yesterday. See, how I am going to take my revenge now that you are going to propose me," said Swetha.

Swetha too agreed and went towards the opposite side of the road. She placed her chunni over her head and then started to walk, swaying her waist, left and right as wide as she can to imitate Bhagyamati.

Then Surya approached Swetha with a royal look and said, "My horse is sick and so I had to come on foot. On the way, I happened to see you. You look so beautiful and have stolen my heart? Who are you, my sweet heart?"

Swetha kept her head towards the ground and slowly raising her eyebrows said, "I am a dancer in this temple. It's time for me to leave for my home as my parents will be waiting. Please give me way."

"Oh my heart's dream, how can you leave me taking away my heart with you? Come with me, I will make you the queen of my heart as well as the Golconda. "

"There is no horse with you now. How can you take me?" asked Swetha, unable to control her laughter and added, "I will come with you only if you bring me the horse."

Surya clapped his hands and there was no response. He clapped his hands once again looking towards Imran and said, "Become a horse, for my sweet heart wants to climb on you."

Imran said, "Teri maaki, you sit on the horse and see how the horse directs you to the Musi River."

"How dare you to speak this way?" responded the Sultan angrily.

"That's more than enough, Sultan. You can expect a national award for your acting skills. Right now, my stomach has got nothing in it and so please, let's go and have something," said Imran, placing his hand over his stomach.

"It's time to have panipuri, then" said Swetha.

"What is panipuri?" said Akanksha.

"It is puri with some pani in it," said Surya.

"Idiot, I didn't ask you," said Akanksha.

"I didn't tell you either."

"What is it Swetha?"

"It is round, hollow, fried bread filled with a mixture of chilly, tamarind, potato, onion, water and few more ingredients."

"If you tell her that way, she is never going to understand it. Give me a chance to explain it to her. Dear Akanksha, please listen carefully. It's a bit difficult to grasp but I will try my best to make you understand. It's like...like... listen carefully... Panipuri for us is like the burger to the west. The only difference is it is a round burger with full of delicious water. The entire structure has to go inside the mouth in the first go itself without spilling the water out. If the water spills out, the taste is gone as it becomes just like any other normal burger. This is the best and the only way one can make you understand," said Surya.

"Nobody on the earth, who has ever tasted it, would explain it as terribly as you did just now. Your poem on Lord Buddha sounds a lot better and creative compared to this one," said Swetha.

"Akanksha, it's better for you to taste it rather than listen to our explanations. Once you taste it, you are never going to leave it," said Swetha

They went to the panipuri shop and everyone was given a specially-designed plate made of some kind of leaf. The person in charge prayed once to Goddess Saraswati picture that was placed beside him and began to serve the panipuri. As soon as the panipuri was placed in the plate, it was being engulfed into their mouth by everyone. Initially, Akanksha found it difficult to place the entire panipuri in her mouth without spilling the water at one go. But due to the continuous efforts of Swetha and Surya, very soon she was able to catch up with the gang and she liked it very much.

They walked debating about the random topics that came across their minds and finally reached the Charminar, the four-pillared love building standing proudly in the city's most busy junction.

It was evening and the pillars looked amazing in the light reddish background caused due to the departure of sun. The pigeons were on their way to Mecca Masjid and some of them took a halt at one of the pillars to have a final look at the sun that had just started embracing the earth. They sang in delight for which the other birds in the nearby trees rushed out and responded with equal vigor and sweetness. Akanksha viewed the historic construction in all the possible directions and appeared to have completely lost in it.

"Amazing! It's one of the best constructions I have ever seen and there is no doubt about it," said Akanksha and added "but the place is not at all maintained. The surroundings are full of dirt and garbage. They should have restricted entry to this place, taken care of it and should have made it better."

"Restricting people is not possible. As far as the people in the old city are concerned, Charminar is not just a tourist spot but something more than that. It is a part of life for everyone here. Without themselves realizing, it has moulded their lives in every possible way it could. It has instilled the values of love and sense of pride in them, by standing there for centuries, representing its urge to move ahead amidst the differences," said Imran.

"Even, I feel like I have got the value of love embracing

and making marks all over me after seeing it. I feel like presenting my loved ones with some memorable gifts so that they become closer to me," said Akanksha.

"Many Hyderabadi Muslims living in Pakistan constructed a replica of Charminar in one of their busy junctions. How they might have been missing this romantic square monument?"

"Yeah, I got to understand it now," said Akanksha.

"They used to allow people to go to the top floor of the minarets, but they stopped it now as failed lovers began to commit suicide from there and many innocent girls were pushed down by their psychotic boyfriends after being rejected for their love," said Swetha.

"Oh, is it?" said Akanksha.

"Do you want to buy bangles? Almost, all the varieties of bangles in the world will be available here," said Swetha to Akanksha.

"Are they good?" said Akanksha.

"How can you ask this question, Akanksha? Why do you think Hyderabad is called the Pearl City? All the world famous love pearls, love bangles and varieties of bangles made of glass and mud will be available here which you won't find anywhere else. Wear a few bangles and a sari and then start to walk. While walking, take care to move your hips like Swetha did when she imitated Bhagyamati and forget not to shake your bangles while you walk. That's it; entire America will shake up and be after you. This is the power of these bangles," said Surya.

7

The Purity of Love

Surya's marriage was to happen in about a week. Everyone was quite excited about going to the coastal region for about 10 days. Moreover, it was the marriage of the ever-smiling member of the gang which added further to the excitement.

Akanksha moved with the parents of Surya. Surya, Siddharth, Imran and Swetha started in a car. Siddharth sat in the driving seat and Swetha sat beside him while Imran and Surya sat on the backseat.

"Within a few days, Surya will no longer be a bachelor," said Swetha.

"I don't like this marriage. I am doing it just for the sake of my parents. I am very much worried about my future and you are adding fuel to my grief."

"You haven't seen her, Surya. What if she is like Sushmitha Sen or Aishwarya Rai?" said Swetha.

"Yeah, Sushmitha and Aishwarya from this village! Siddharth, why did you bring Swetha here? She is going to use this as an opportunity to kill me during the entire journey with her stupid questions. You should have sent her with Akanksha."

Siddharth smiled and said, "Don't you think girls like Sushmitha Sen and Aishwarya can't be found in the villages?"

"There might be. That is the reason why I have been imagining a lot about the way she looks. If you say Sushmitha and Aishwarya, my expectations peak up and finally when I see the real one, I might not like her."

"So what all did you imagine about her?" said Swetha

"Swetha, I beg you. Please leave this topic," said Surya.

"So, you are not going to tell all your imaginations."

"Not at all, especially to you," said Surya.

"Did you invite your Sandhya, Saroja, Sushmitha, Madhumitha and all the other ex-es?"

"I have given them the invitation and it's up to them to decide. I don't think anyone would come so far."

While the conversation was going on, they came across some wires hanging on the road beside a transformer. The wires looked like the snakes passing between the trees. Siddharth stopped the car and everyone got out of the car.

"What happened?" asked Swetha.

"Electrical break down due to strong wind or some kind of storm, I guess" replied Surya.

"What shall we do now?" asked Swetha.

"We all have got Engineering degrees. Someone among us must do something," said Imran.

"Your mother tells entire Hyderabad about your Engineering degree. You are the most eligible among us to do something Imran," said Surya.

"Yes, Imran, the Engineer! Please do something and see that the car moves."

"What on earth do I know about these wires hanging here?"

"You have an Engineering degree which your mother is extremely proud of. What on earth do you require more than that to do?"

"I sat behind Surya in all the exams and managed to pass in 2nd class. Surya passed in 1st class, so ask him to do something."

"Saroja has passed in distinction and so I landed up in 1st class. All I know is to arrange the required books for her so that she does the remaining work," said Surya.

"May be the transformer has blast off," said Siddharth.

"You better stick to the exploitations and world

revolutions, Siddharth. Else there are going to be blasts everywhere," said Surya.

"I remember, Swetha always used to do most amazing things in the labs and she can only rescue us."

"What Siddharth said is right. The transformer might have blast off and we can't do anything with our Mechanical degrees. All we need is an Electrical Engineer."

"Your mind is also spoiled by staying with Siddharth," said Surya.

"What happened?"

"If a transformer blasts off, why the hell would be the wires hanging on the road. Everything would have blown to pieces," said Surya.

"Transformer burst! Everything blown to pieces! I told you guys not to watch many action movies," said Imran and added "let me try something."

Imran went forward like the hero does in South Indian movies and as he moved forward to hold the wires, "Imran!" screamed Swetha.

"What happened?" asked Imran.

"Did you wear your shoe? I remember one of our professors saying that it protects you from the electrical shocks."

"Yeah, the same professor sent me out of the lab for not wearing the shoe."

"May be you can use a wooden stick to lift the wires so that it protects you from an electrical shock," said Swetha.

Imran searched for a stick and as soon as he found it, reached near the wires. There was panic everywhere and all of them were eagerly waiting to watch the consequences. Imran held the wires with the stick and carefully lifted the wires as Siddharth started the car and passed beneath it.

"Hail Imran, the engineer," shouted everyone.

"They are just like the normal wires found in our houses but weren't looking so probably because of their location amidst the forest chaos. Anyway, the credit should go to Swetha. She is the one who reminded me of the stick," said Imran.

"Yeah, credit should go to Swetha for coming up with the wonderful idea of recruiting Electrical Engineer for lifting the wires," said Surya.

"My idea is lot better than your theory of `everything blasting to pieces'."

"It is you and Siddharth who gave me the idea by saying that the transformer would have burst," said Imran.

The criticism of one another continued for about another half an hour till they reached a waterfall on the way. Everyone was quite exhausted and they thought that the view of the scenic beauty could lift their moods and so they headed there. They had to climb a small hill to get the complete view of the waterfall. With much effort, they reached the view point where their effort bore fruits as it was very pleasant and the cool breeze mesmerized them. This sort of climate was completely new to them and so, for a while, they became children and played in the downpour.

While they were on their way down the hill, they came across a little boy of around 10 years and a younger girl of about five years. The boy was selling amlas in a small basket while the little girl sat beside her brother watching him sell the fruits.

"How much does it cost?" asked Swetha catching the cheek of the young one.

"Five for a rupee."

"Won't you give six for a rupee?" asked Swetha.

"No, madam."

"Okay. Give me 25," said Swetha with a smile.

"He handed over 25 amlas and Siddharth took a 10-rupee note from his pocket and gave him."

The boy took five one-rupee coins from his pocket to return it to Siddharth when

Swetha said, "Keep the money with you, chotu."

"The boy with utter innocence evident in his eyes returned back the coins telling, "I don't take money without a reason, madam."

"Take it, chotu. He is just like your bother," said Swetha.

"No, madam. If you want to give me that five rupees,

take 25 more amlas or else, I can polish sir's shoes," he said.

"Okay fine, never mind it. Don't you go to school?" Siddharth asked.

"No."

"Why don't you?"

"My school teacher should be given grains of rice or vegetables or fruits. Else, he doesn't allow the students. We ourselves don't have anything to eat and how can we give him? He started beating me since I didn't give him anything for two weeks. It was very difficult to bear him. I told my mother that I will stop going to school and she agreed. I like plucking these fruits from the trees and selling them. The first day I earned some money and gave them to my mother, she was very delighted and so I wanted to continue it. I am also earning some money by polishing shoes. I can be a guide too. One day, I want to take my mother to a Chiranjeevi movie in the town."

"What does your father do?" asked Siddharth.

"Why do you ask about him, brother? He will always be in the toddy shop. At night he comes home, scolds mother and then beats her without any reason. Poor mother weeps all night. I would have gone to town like my friend who earns some money there but for the sake of my mother, I remain here."

They snapped a photograph with the children and showed the picture to them. The children were extremely delighted and surprised.

"What is your name, chotu?"

"Chiru," replied the boy.

"So you are the Mega Star," said Swetha.

"Yes madam. In the entire village, I am the only one who knows the entire list of Chiru's films, right from his first movie till now. I am a very big fan of Chiru. My actual name is something else, but I forgot it ever since I left the school. Now my name is fixed as Chiru. All my friends and everyone in the village call me as Chiru and I like it very much," he said proudly.

"So what is your name, sweet heart?" asked Swetha.

"Manasa," said the girl in her sweet breaking voice.

They bade them good bye and returned to the car. The plight of the boy and the girl touched everyone and they remained silent in the car.

"Since morning, how much have we wasted? All the mineral water bottles, pizzas, the biryani and what not. We are wasting the food here while these children are struggling hard for every penny. It really makes me feel ashamed. What have the children done? Why should they suffer so much? Is there no end to all this? Who would solve their problem? When will their messiah come? See his poor mother, everyday her animal husband is torturing her. No one protects her from her cruel husband. All that everyone has to say is, she has been tied the knot by her husband and she has to stay with him forever. She doesn't know any law or any right. All that she does is get beaten up and cry all night. When will the end come for these family tyrants? What are all the social organizations doing? They do hell a lot of useless activities in cities. Don't they have the moral responsibility for the name they bear? What is the government doing? Does it bother only about the deficit budgets? Doesn't it have any other responsibility? Sixty years of independence and where are we still? Marriage, I don't know understand what they get by marriage. As soon as the girl becomes 16, they will give her to some bloody brute of same class and caste. The whole society murmurs if she is in her family after a certain age. Hell with this society. All those beautiful smiles of the girls are shattered with the entry of the monstrous marriage. In the name of marriage, they leave their homes getting ready for all the problems," said Siddharth in a very emotional manner.

Swetha went beside Siddharth, caught his hand, placed her head over his shoulder and said, "The world runs this way. Leave it, Siddharth. Don't think too much about it. We are going to Surya's marriage."

There was complete silence for the rest of the journey and, finally, they reached the destination and went for sleep right away.

The next morning, everyone was ready to go to the marriage place. Swetha was ready by 8 AM and came to wake Siddharth up who was still asleep.

Siddharth unwillingly opened his eyes and said, "You guys can leave. I will go to the village for an hour or two and then catch you guys later."

"What happened? Is everything alright?" enquired Surya.

"He still has that boy and the girl in his mind. Let him go to the village for some sightseeing which might freshen him up. Let's go ahead," said Swetha.

"Swetha!" said Siddharth.

"What happened?"

"You look very good in this sari."

"Thanks, Siddharth."

"Sorry for stopping you guys in the middle of the romantic conversation, Siddharth. It's already late and so we are moving and will be waiting for you," said Surya.

Akanksha, by then, came there in an auto and met them as they just started out in the car.

She saw Swetha in sari and said, "I have never worn a sari till now. See how beautiful Swetha is looking. There is a sari in my luggage which I had kept in your car yesterday. I hesitated to wear it but Surya's mother is insisting me to wear it. After seeing Swetha in a sari, I got enough courage and feel like wearing it."

"Let's see who is going to be the centre of attraction whether it's you or Swetha," said Surya.

"How can I ever be better than Swetha? Stop your comparisons and tell me where you have kept my luggage."

"The luggage is in the corner room. Shall we wait for you?" asked Surya.

"Your mom and dad are waiting for you. I can return back in the same auto. You guys may proceed," she said and added "by the way, where is Siddharth?"

"His mood is not good. He is still asleep," said Swetha and continued, "if he wakes up by then, you can come with him. We will meet you guys there."

She went inside and found Siddharth still sleeping. She went to the corner room, searched for the luggage, found the sari in it and then went to the bathroom to have a shower. She had her bath and then came out to her room. She could observe Siddharth still sleeping, his face facing towards her room. She stared at him for a while and suddenly some devilish thoughts creeped into her mind. She went into the bathroom to have shower once again and began to sing in the hope of waking him up. She came out wearing a towel to find Siddharth still fast asleep. She kept the door of her room open and then turned away from Siddharth, removed her towel and stood there completely naked for a while. Her hands and legs trembled, her heart started beating as fast as it could and, soon, she started sweating. She then slowly made up her mind and turned back to find Siddharth still asleep. She then thought of making some noises to wake him up but stopped herself from getting desperate.

Now with the door still open, she covered the lower part of her body, exposing her top part. She started wearing her blouse, but the devil wouldn't leave her. She looked back to see Siddharth in the same position but couldn't resist now. She unhooked all the buttons, took a glass that was on the table and then, dropped it. Thinking that the chance would not come again, she unbuttoned the hook of her inner wear again and dropped the glass again and uttered the word 'Siddharth' loudly turning to the other side so that her bare back was visible to Siddharth.

She could hear Siddharth wake up now. Somehow, she drew the courage to speak and said, "Siddharth, please help me in buttoning these hooks. It is very difficult as this is the first time I am trying to wear a sari and there is no one left to help me."

Siddharth was initially reluctant to go towards her but after seeing her bare back, fully exposing the tiny drops of water slowly but reluctantly trying to part from her body, the devil in him too woke up and he went towards her.

Akanksha still trying to button the hooks once again said, "Siddharth, please help me."

Siddharth approached her slowly. Now her entire bare wheatish back was exposed before him. He caught the two corners of the blouse and tried to pull the ends to hook them but stopped after hearing a painful sound from Akanksha. Again he tried to move them closer, this time a bit slower and, in the process, his hands touched her back. With this touch, Akanksha couldn't resist further and moved towards him. She looked straight into his eyes, took his hand, placed it over her waist and said, "You remember, you asked me the meaning of my name. It means 'Desire.' My parents kept it since they wanted me to conquer whatever I desired for. The first day I saw you, you have become my desire and I knew that the doors of my heart opened for you."

While listening to her, Siddharth realized his hand sliding over her curvy waist ultimately landing on her lower waist. Her top was now fully visible to him. He couldn't resist as her lips moved towards his. He placed his hands around her bosom to feel them. He then embraced her and moved towards her as his lips locked into hers. Just as Akanksha too started to enter the mysterious wild world, he suddenly moved away from her as if some current had passed him.

"What happened?" said Akanksha taking his hand and placing them over her bosom again.

Siddharth removed his hands and said, "I am extremely sorry for this, Akanksha. Please forgive me."

"What's wrong?"

"I can't do this, Akanksha. I simply can't do it."

"For a while, there was wonderful chemistry between us and all of a sudden what happened to you?"

"You have got beautiful curves and wonderful face. Every man in the world would love to make love to you."

"Then, what's wrong with you?"

"There is some hidden force that's stopping me from doing it. As I proceeded further, the images of Swetha flashed over my mind and I couldn't do it. She is all pure and is patiently waiting for me. I can't do it, Akanksha. Her pureness is stopping me from doing it. Please forgive me for everything," said Siddharth and left.

Akanksha couldn't speak anything. She felt humiliated. She now closed the door, changed her dress, kept the sari in the bag and wore jean and T-shirt. She came out like a lost soul, sat on the steps and started weeping like a child keeping her head down.

Siddharth came towards her and said, "I am sorry, Akanksha, if I have hurt you."

Akanksha didn't speak anything.

"Please speak something, Akanksha."

She slowly raised her head and said, "I am extremely sorry for what I did. Please forget what all has happened now. We will be as we were before. I am leaving for the marriage."

She then cleared all her tears, came out to sit in the auto and left for the marriage.

CHAPTER

The Marriage

Akanksha reached the venue of marriage. The canopy and the surroundings were fully decorated with auspicious leaves. Everyone was busy with the marriage arrangements. The atmosphere was very pleasant. New relationships were being formed. Old bonds were to be strengthened. It was a grand get-together for the old. They were sitting in groups and talking about their own marriages and post-marriage lives. There were smiles everywhere. New introductions were taking place. Stories were being exchanged and intermingling of cultures was taking place. Young boys were busy in their hunt for cute girls. Teenage girls in their traditional dresses were keenly observing the hunters following them. Children were on cloud nine now as they were away from their schools and there seemed to be no boundaries for their happiness.

Surya was getting dressed in the green room and was feeling very tensed as was clearly evident from his face. Swetha and Imran were with him.

"You are going to see your sweetheart in a few minutes. How is your heart beating?" asked Swetha.

"Do you remember Subramanian, our maths sir? How the heart used to beat whenever we had to face him? I am feeling the same now. I have been with many girls but I was never afraid so much!"

"Subramanian sir! Don't remind me of him. I had enough nightmares about him," said Swetha and added "so you are very much afraid now."

"Of course, I am, Swetha."

"How are you going to deal then? What will be the first line that you are going to speak to her?"

"Let me gather enough courage to look into her eyes. Then I can think of talking to her."

"What if she looks like Aishwarya Rai or Sushmitha Sen?"

"Aishwarya and Sushmitha... from this village!"

"Why not? There will be many beautiful girls in the villages. Okay, how do you expect her to be?"

"If she is average in looks like you, that's enough for me."

"Am I average?"

"Definitely."

"Really!"

"No sweetheart. You are the best. She can never be like you. Even if she is so, she can never be as understanding as you are," said Surya.

"What if she is fat and ugly?"

"Please don't frighten me, Swetha."

Akanksha came there and Swetha noticed her and said, "Surya, I am leaving the room. Akanksha has come and we both will have a look around."

"Please don't do that, Swetha. Be with me till I leave the room. I will be comfortable if you are with me."

"Okay, don't worry. I am staying back," replied Swetha and turning towards Akanksha asked, "Why didn't you wear the sari?"

"It's Indian thing and didn't fit me well."

"It's not that it didn't fit you. It fits for everyone. You just didn't know how to wear it. Shall I try it for you?"

"It's okay, Swetha. I am comfortable in jeans."

"It's okay then. Where have you been all the time?"

"I came here long back. I am completely new to village life and so was wandering to have a feel of the village."

"What about Siddharth? Did he wake up?"

"I don't know. When I was returning, he was still asleep. But it was long back."

"Okay," said Swetha as they moved towards the mandapam along with Surya.

Surya sat near the purohit and as soon as he sat, the purohit started reciting the mantras.

Akanksha and Swetha were standing behind Surya.

"You like Siddharth so much, right?" Akanksha asked Swetha.

"Yeah, very much. Why do you ask me now?"

"Just out of curiosity. He's strange."

The bride entered with a coconut in her hands and was accompanied by a few young girls. She walked slowly towards the canopy, keeping her head down.

Surya had never seen her before. Neither had he seen her photograph. She was now standing before him with her hands extended. Surya looked at her hands. They were slim and fair. She sat beside him on the advice of the purohit. As soon as she sat next to him, Surya's heart skipped a beat. He could now see her hands clearly and felt like touching them. He tried in vain to have a look at her face without moving his head but couldn't succeed though there was only a foot distance between them. At the same time, the bride was also trying to have a glimpse of her hero. She moved her plaited hair back and, in the process, looked sideward to get a quick glimpse of Surya. Was it because of their own marriage experience or because of the experience of attending so many marriages or because of the fact that they have observed the efforts of the pair to view each other, nobody knows, but the elder women, who stood behind them came forward and tried to bridge the gap between them. In the process, both their shoulders touched. The touch fuelled Surya and gave him enough courage due to which he moved slowly towards her and touched her shoulder with his own. The bride also didn't move her shoulder away and she too seemed to enjoy the romantic touch. Both of them were oblivious of the world that was around them and couldn't hear anymore mantras. Like the lustful lips that approach for the first time and stick without parting, their shoulders remained in contact for the next few minutes. The heat generated by the touch fuelled Surya further and with little force, he moved her shoulder with his own. She responded similarly, satisfying the Newton's third law and with this, Surya got the signal he was waiting for. He couldn't resist now looking at her and raised his head slowly to have a look at her. Surya couldn't understand how it was communicated to her because, at the same moment, she too looked at him. As the lotus opens up with the arrival of the sun, she opened her eyes wide to have a view of Surya and in a split second, she closed her eyes and moved her head down. Their eyes were in contact just for a second but they could see their entire future in that second.

"How did you meet Siddharth, Swetha?" asked Akanksha.

"We were together since childhood. We studied in the same school and my dad worked as a teacher there. Siddharth was a bright, honest and silent guy. He used to respect everyone and used to address the grievances of the students. His qualities appealed to everyone and so he was chosen as the representative. Our teachers loved him the most, my dad being the foremost among them. Siddharth used to ask questions both academic and non-academic that used to surprise my dad. He wrote poems that used to touch everyone. Most of his poems were in lucid language and dealt with the poor and their lives. He used to worry whenever he used to see the poor on the streets. He is not like us who just feel bad for the poor but he has really developed a great desire to do something for them. The depth of his qualities and the breadth of his mind attracted me towards him," said Swetha.

Surya stood, held the sacred thread in his hands and with the instructions given by purohit, lowered his body to tie the knot while the bride remained seated in the same place. Women standing behind her lifted her plaited hair and Surya tied the three knots.

"How did you guys come to like each other?"

"I never talked to people then. I was short-tempered and used to be alone. People felt that I was proud and never used to talk to me. All this made me look unique and Siddharth got attracted to me. He used to gaze at me and looked for opportunities to be with me. He used to talk to me though the situation did not demand. He showed special interest on my birthdays. He always used to know my likes and made sure to use them on special occasions to gift me. He used to come to my home to talk to my dad but sometimes I felt that he used it as an opportunity to talk to me. Sometimes, he used to start some conversation, feel tensed, change the topic and talk something which didn't make any sense. He never paid attention to any other girl. He was very different and interesting. He studied well and was very good at mathematics. If there is anything that I am afraid of, it is mathematics. One day, an inspector visited our school and due to my behavior, I became his main target and asked me to prepare well for a chapter called 'limits' on which he would ask the questions a week later. On my dad's advice, I approached Siddharth to clear my concepts. He tried to explain me in the simplest manner possible but my mind was not ready for mathematics. The next day, he gave me a folded paper. When I opened it, I found something written on it. I thought and wished it to be a love letter. In fact, it was a love letter but was in a completely different style and format. 'Experiencing the limit' was the title and it followed this way.

Experiencing the limit

My mind is not interested in anything. Its focus is only you. It wants to know only about you. So I started knowing about you. I thought about you, dreamt about you. I thought I knew you. I wanted to convey my feelings to you. I came to tell you and there again, I saw you and I found something more in you. I somehow feel I know much less about you. And then again I think about you, dream about you. It is 'I know you' and 'I don't know you' at the same time. This reminds me of my difficulty in explaining the concept of limit in mathematics to you. Now I am experiencing it. You are my 'limit' since you are 'limitless.' There is always something more to feel about you.

Thus, he expressed his desire. I liked him very much but I was not clear about my decision which might be because of my age then. I kept the letter with me but didn't respond to him. I used to read it every day and used to recall it whenever I saw him. Though it was a mathematical love letter, it never bored me and till now, it is the most cherished present, I have ever received.

After that, I tried to spend most of my time with him but I never talked to him about the letter or my answer to him though it was conveyed indirectly to him. He too didn't force me to reply for the same. He told me that those were his real heart-felt feelings. He liked me the most and was pretty clear about it.

I knew that he was the right one for me but didn't reveal anything to him about my desires. Time proceeded but nothing changed between us. We used to love each other's company. It was after four years he gave me the letter, I read it out to my dad on my birthday and discussed it with him. He had no objection as it was Siddharth. The next day, I met Siddharth and told him that I also liked him."

Surya, with his finger locked to that of the bride, started walking the seven sacred steps around the sacred fire which signified the seven vows of commitment for each other.

"See the way Surya is pretending to be decent before his wife. One day I should tell his wife about all he did before the marriage."

"And then what happened afterwards?" asked Akanksha as if she was not interested in the marriage that was going on.

"What happened?" enquired Swetha.

"I mean to say what happened after you said that you liked Siddharth?"

"I used to be arrogant since my childhood and even my dad used to say this. I hated this male-dominated society and thought that a married woman loses freedom. I had my own explanations and interpretations for my beliefs and ego. I was living in a world of virtual happiness but with the entry of Siddharth in my life, my priorities have changed. The way I looked at things changed and I felt the changes that were happening in me. My tastes, my ambitions, my outlook towards life changed and I cherished each and every moment I spent with him. If you don't think it a bit dramatizing, I could see heaven on earth. I have liberty, independence and there are people who understand me and appreciate my thoughts. All I want now is to be with Siddharth and be a part of whatever he does. I tell you one thing, Akanksha, if you are not bored."

"I am not at all bored. I am highly impressed," said Akanksha.

Swetha continued, "You can never know a person completely. It is an infinite process. The process in getting to know the person is most interesting as everyday would be a new learning. If the process is to get to know a person whom you like the most, it is then you experience love. The same is written in the letter to me by Siddharth and the same is being experienced by me. The moment you enter this interesting process, the worldly desires automatically die down and life becomes very meaningful."

"What are your plans for your future now?" asked Akanksha.

"Siddharth encouraged me to do whatever I liked. I too had many plans but all my aims seemed narrow compared to his. The world of Siddharth is amazing. It is full of adventures with a humanitarian look as the main focus of it. He wants to become a son for the old, brother for the poor and father of an orphan. I just want to be his companion and his wife. I love this life and as of now, being with the loved one is enough for me. His love for people, desire to know things, continuous thinking to find solutions for a better world bound me to him. This, in fact, happens to everyone who is with him. The more one knows him, the less he wants to lose him," said Swetha.

CHAPTER

9

Fun in the Village

Surya's marriage ceremony was finally over. People were now relaxing and discussing about the highlights of the marriage. New relations were formed and new friendships blossomed. The place was full of energy with elderly debates and children's games.

Four girls, belonging to the bride's group, wearing traditional *langa voni's* and moving their plaited hair synchronously to the tunes of their waists came and stopped near Imran. They stared at him for a while with a strange look on their faces.

"They might be the bride's friends," whispered Swetha.

"So you are the Nizam boys, who have come *all the way* from the capital," said one of the girls bringing her plaited hair towards her front and swirling it around her finger.

"There are many who came all the way from Hyderabad and we are a few among them," said Imran stressing the word 'all the way.'

"Did you see our Megastar Chiranjeevi in Hyderabad?" asked the girl while the other three girls laughed.

"I saw his brother Pawan Kalyan too," said Imran and added "do you need anything else?"

"Nothing," said the girl and started moving away.

She returned back now swinging her waist as much as she can and said, "We saw a guitar in the bridegroom's hand. Does he really play it or is it just to impress our girl?"

"It is not Surya who brought it. I brought it to impress cute girls like you," said Imran trying to counter them who were dominating him.

"Aha! To impress cute girls like us," said the girl and continued, "Should I tell the same to Nasreen?"

Hearing the name of Nasreen, everyone was shocked. Imran couldn't control further and said, "How do you know Nasreen?"

The girls laughed uncontrollably and then took out a greeting card which was supposed to be from Nasreen to Imran.

Imran pleaded with the girls and finally took it from them. 'I miss you so much' was the only sentence written and after reading that Imran couldn't control his emotions and was on cloud nine for a while.

"She misses you so much I guess. You should have brought her here," said one of the girls while the others laughed.

"Even I am missing her so much," replied Imran,

"You see how Imran plays guitar for us now," said Swetha.

"I was just kidding. Surya is the one who plays the guitar. Go and ask your bride groom to play the guitar," said Imran and continued, "By the way, how did you get this greeting card?"

The girls again laughed uncontrollably and said, "How do we get it? The postman is the one who gives the post. Don't you know it?"

"It's okay, baba. Thank you very much," said Imran.

"Thanks! Just thanks!"

"Okay, soon there will be my marriage with Nasreen. I will show you girls everything in the capital city if you come to Hyderabad for my marriage. I will also let you taste the Hyderabadi Biryani," said Imran.

"Whatever be the topic, Hyderabadi Biryani is sure to come when Imran speaks," said Swetha.

"Hyderabadi Biryani deserves it," said Imran.

"Ok sure, we will come to Hyderabad, meet you there and see your Nasreen too," said the girls and as they moved waving good bye, Imran interrupted them and said, "Can you show us the village now? We heard from stories that village beauty magnifies if we see it with the cute village girls."

"Aha! Is it? Anyways, today there will be dramas and so we cannot accompany you. We can do one thing. We will request a few young men to accompany you who know the village well. Is it ok for you?" replied the girls.

"We would have been very happy if you girls would have accompanied us but, anyway, since you have got some work, we will proceed with anyone you send with us," said Imran.

Swetha and Akanksha liked the idea and quickly agreed. The girl in the *langa voni* went and came with a group of four young boys. Two of them were wearing T-shirt and the other two wore shirts but all of them were wearing the famous *lungi*. The lungi seemed to be the most famous attire here as everyone from the age of 10 to 60 was seen to be wearing it. The leader of the group was Malli, who had two long, protruding teeth on the front and looked funny when he smiled. He was very excited since he was requested by the beauty of the village to accompany her guests.

"Okay, madams. What do you want to see?" asked Malli.

"Everything that is not found in the city," said Swetha.

"Everything you see here will not be found except the second-hand buses that are sent after you people have used them in the cities," said Malli and added, "I will try to show as many places as possible but I can do that only till the drama time. By the time the drama starts, we need to be here."

The first place they went to was the sea. The sea shore was unlike the famous beaches of India. There were very few people and among them, most were the fishermen busy repairing their boats.

A group of young boys seeing Akanksha in her jeans

whistled at her. Malli responded strongly. The boys didn't pay attention to him and whistled again passing bad comments.

Malli got irritated by now and said, "You idiots! You don't have enough courage to face us and how dare you insult our guests?"

"Look who is talking about the courage," was the response.

"Common let's have a fight today," said an excited Malli.

Akanksha was observing all this and the young blood in the group couldn't wait anymore and so they too retaliated in the same tone.

"Let's have a fight in the sea and pray to God for your unfulfilled wish, for today is your end. Let's see who will save you," said one among them,

"Why the sea? Let's have it on the land where you are born. If your balls haven't got enough courage, let's see who climbs the coconut trees fast and break the fruits," said Malli.

"Come to the sea if you want to fight or else leave from here wearing the bangles our sweetheart is wearing," said one among the group pointing his finger towards Akanksha, as the others laughed loudly. They went into the waters and giving a flying kiss to Akanksha shouted, "Sweet heart. We love you. Come here. We will show you how to swim."

"Idiots! How dare you comment on our guest? Don't forget that you come to the market some day. We will see your end there," said Malli.

"When we are here, why talk about market, you gutless creature," came the voice.

Malli didn't stop and went on uttering words but they reached very far where the tides couldn't be seen.

"Why are they asking you guys to fight in the sea?" asked Swetha.

"They are the lower caste people who depend on the sea for their livelihood. Sea is like mother to them. Since their birth, they stay most of the time in the sea than on the land. It's like they have a great deal of control over it and derive strength from it. They can fight as well as swim at the same time but for us it is difficult in the sea. We can't swim like them and fighting while swimming is extremely difficult. If they come to the land, we will show them what we are," said Malli and continued, "Madam. These fights are common to us. Don't take their comments to heart. Forget everything and have a nice dip. The weather is very good today. Would you like to have a dip?"

"No," said Imran.

"Wait for a few minutes. We will have a dip and return," said Malli and left with his gang into the water.

Siddharth could see them going far. He tried to compare the styles of swimming of both groups. He couldn't find any and was equally impressed by their skills. They had their bath and returned. While they were about to leave, Swetha asked Malli, "What are you studying now?"

"We did our schooling till seventh as we have school only till that after which we have to travel far. Leaving our parents alone, we can't go there. Some private schools are heaping up nowadays but they are very expensive. After our seventh exams, most of us stop going to school since we cannot afford to join these private schools. Only one or two get through the seventh board exams in distinction and manage to go farther places to study."

"What about girls?"

"They have to end their studies even if they pass the exams with very good marks."

"Are the private schools very expensive?"

"Yeah, they are mainly for the children of railway employees and the government employees. But nowadays, people are admitting their children in the private schools even though the fee is high as these untouchables you have just seen are being admitted into the government schools. It is difficult to sit with them. We don't even invite them to our marriages," said Malli.

While telling this, Malli never felt at any point of time that he was talking something wrong. He seemed to be so convinced and proud of the richness of his blood the caste had given him. With great confidence he told this, thinking that everyone in the bridegroom's batch would be from a higher caste as the bride was from a higher caste. When people get convinced that you are a member of their group, it is then that their true intention and thoughts are disclosed. Otherwise, all that we get are encrypted messages. As these kinds of caste and religion-based ideas were still being observed in the cities where most were educated, it wasn't strange to hear them from the villagers.

Malli knew every nook and corner of the village and showed his guests all the places. Siddharth and the batch also seemed to enjoy everything that was shown to them. They walked through the green fields trying to catch the goats, plucked different varieties of flowers, drank fresh toddy, travelled in boats, plucked lotus from the ponds, went behind the buffaloes with a stick, plucked fresh fruits, took photographs with the tribals, visited the old village temples, travelled in the bullock carts and sat on the top of the only village bus.

When the sun had almost gone down and started embracing the earth, Malli said, "Madam, the drama might have started already. The dances follow the drama and I don't want to miss them. I have shown you most of the places to be seen here but if you feel like seeing something more we can come again tomorrow."

"It's okay. We will return back. We also want to see the drama," said Swetha.

On their way back, they came across a canal and Malli said, "The boating races take place here during Sankranti. It is really wonderful to see the race as many skilled boatmen from other villages come to participate here but it is we who win the race most of the time."

By the time they reached home, the drama 'Pandava Vanavasam' had come to an end. People were very much immersed in it as was clearly evident from their faces. Tears were flowing out from the women's eyes seeing the plight of the heroes in their favorite epic.

Young were eagerly waiting for the song session which was to take place soon. As soon as the curtains drew on the drama, a person, with a mike in hand, came forward to announce the next event.

He slowly raised his voice amidst the cheers that followed his entry and announced, "The time for which you have been waiting eagerly has come finally. The next event depicts the romance between a *baava* and his *maradalu*."

At this juncture, a young man with four other young men and a girl with four other young women entered the scene amidst the clapping and cheers of the villagers.

"Two of the girls were with us in the morning!" said Imran.

"Yeah, these are the same girls who brought the letter," responded Swetha.

The girls swaying their waists neatly to the tunes of the music and tapping their feet to the ground sang...

Female: O bava, O bava...

Male: Tell me dear, o my dear...

Female: You took me here and you took me there. Now that, every tree knows us and every bush feels us, where will you take me?

O bava, my dear bava...

Male: Those trees die down and the bushes die down.

I take you to my heart where you live forever.

O maradala, my dear maradala...

Female: You touch me here and you touch me there.

 You kiss me here and you kiss me there.

 It's wrong, bava, O bava...

Male: When I touch you, I forget the world

When I kiss you, I forget the God

What is wrong and what is right?

O maradala, my dear maradala...

Thus the romance between the childhood sweethearts ended with good steps to the tunes of the folk music with folk lyrics. Amidst the claps, the curtains came down. The Nizam group recalled their school days where they played the folk songs in their school day celebrations. The folk tale, their costumes, their expression, the villagers' reaction, etc impressed them.

"Surya did a similar folk song in school," said Swetha.

"Oh, I didn't know it. Do you have any pictures?" asked Akanksha.

"Yeah, I have it in my album. I too did a solo performance. I will show you all of them as soon as we reach Hyderabad," said Swetha.

The announcer again came forward after the curtain was closed, "I hope you all enjoyed the romantic tale. Now it's time to weep, care and feel pity. Here is the girl who is depressed at her lover's departure and is eagerly waiting for him."

The curtain raised and a young girl immersed in deep thoughts was sitting under a tree. As the tempo of the music started building up, she started singing.

Oh, my dear cloud…
Where has my loved one gone?
He told me he would return with all his presents.
Is he the one who has sent you with accumulated wealth in your heart?
Did he tell you to shower them over me?
No, my dear cloud…
Tell him that I want him and not his gifts.
Oh my dear air,
You smell sweet today.
Your touch strengthens me today.
I know that you are coming from him.
I feel you as my close companion.
Please my dear friend, convey all my feelings to him.
Tell him my eyes have stopped blinking in search of him.
Oh my dear moon,
You have come back but I find no glory in you.
All your beauty is lost without him near me.
You are the one who witnessed all our love
How can you come leaving him somewhere?
Bring him back and come back with all your glory of combining the loved ones.

The curtains closed slowly. The sweetness of Telugu language with so many heart-touching words combined with the beautiful expressions of the girl touched everyone and most of them were still in the lost world of the lover.

"That is the reason why they call it 'Italian of the east'.

What can be more soothing than hearing the Telugu language? Had Veturi been here, his heart would have been delighted with joy after watching this," said Siddharth.

"After hearing this, I too feel like listening to Veturi, Cinare and Athreya," said Swetha.

"Who are these Veturi, Cinare and Athreya?" asked Akanksha.

"They are the saviors of the Telugu language who have been trying to strengthen the light of the candle which has been in the decay," said Siddharth.

The atmosphere became calm after the love song and the announcer again came forward, this time the glow in his eyes was clearly evident.

"Dear villagers, I know you are immersed so much in the tale of the lost lover. Please wake up from the beds of isolation. Manga is waiting for you, me and for the entire village."

To this announcement, the energy in the youth woke up and the old also were equally energized and started smiling. The curtain slowly raised to give the stage to Manga.

Manga sat on the stage, slowly removed the cloth that covered her face, opened her eyes and sang moving her lips slowly as the music started.

"O dear bava's and my dear mava's
My eyes are paining, my cheeks are paining and my hands are paining
My waist is paining, my legs are paining
In fact, my entire body is paining
I went to the doctor in search of medicine.
He looked at all the places, gave all the injections and said…
and said…

She began to smile.

"What did he say?" someone from the crowd asked.

He said these injections are not sufficient to cure my weakness and
Advised me to insert all the village injections to get cured.
And so I came here…

At this juncture, the whole crowd started dancing and whistling, fully out of their senses.

O bava's, O mava's
Remember the last full moon day
When the moon light became my dress
When we were locked together
When the air between us couldn't breathe
 When our ages couldn't sleep further
In search of all of them I came here
O bava's, my mava's..

The crowd was dancing madly, trying to reach Manga and in the process were falling on one another. Amidst this unconscious state of the crowd, the curtain closed.

While they were on their way back, Akanksha said, "The last song lyrics were very bad and I couldn't hear it. How can people dance so wildly to these kinds of songs? How are the women able to see it? They too seemed to enjoy the song. "

"I too didn't like the content but it has energy. I had no problem in seeing as I got used to these sort of songs," said Swetha.

Siddharth intervened and said, "We didn't like it but that is how mass songs are supposed to be. It is not only the men, but the women too were happy, looking at their respective men reacting to the song. All these songs with their outcomes are taken for granted. With all our scriptures, fully of characters of these kinds, you should naturally expect people to accept this kind of songs and dance to them."

"It might have appealed to them but I didn't like it. I liked the first one where the love birds romanced," said Akanksha.

"The first one is a bit routine and has got no lyrical strength but the performance was good. I liked the second one where everything was perfectly blended," said Swetha.

"I too liked the second one," said Siddharth.

"It's natural," said Akanksha.

"Why is it natural?" asked Siddharth.

"Nothing," said Akanksha.

"I liked the last one. It was full of energy and I felt like dancing to it. If Surya would have been there, he would have given me company but, unfortunately, he is not here ," said Imran.

"Which song did you like, Malli?" asked Swetha.

"Definitely the last one, didn't you see me how I fell thrice trying to catch her. I almost touched her hand once," said Malli.

The debate went on till they reached the house. They thanked Malli and the group, had a snap with them and bade them goodbye.

10
CHAPTER

The Sweet Heart

In the moon-lit night, they placed the thread cots in the open space in front of the house and sat down to chat for a while. The view of the full moon among the randomly spread stars and the birds calling their loved ones amidst the soothing sound made by the palm trees completely mesmerized all of them.

"The village is very good. Altogether, it has shown me a different world," said Akanksha.

"Yeah for me too," said Swetha opening her mouth wide with a deep breath.

"Are you feeling sleepy?"

"Yeah, sort of."

"People are here to share their village experiences. Don't you want to hear them?" said Akanksha.

"I am very tired today. I will hear them tomorrow and share my experience too. Good night everyone," said Swetha sleeping on the cot and placing her hand around Siddharth who was facing Akanksha and Imran.

"Good night," replied everyone as Swetha closed her eyes.

"What if I choose this as my place, Imran? This place is exactly like the place I wished to go to. It is a place full of rich civilization and age-old traditions but completely cut off from the modern world. Each one in the village has got the potential of earning a decent life but is leading a very pathetic life. Pathetic doesn't mean they are unhappy but have got adjusted and satisfied with their livelihood. If they know their rights and come to know about the available opportunities, they can really make very good fortune," said Siddharth.

"Yes, this place is very good and, in a short time, we came to know many people which would be of great help. You wouldn't feel lonely here," said Imran.

"Will you accompany me?" asked Siddharth.

"Me!" exclaimed Imran.

"Yeah."

"I cannot do it and you know about it, Siddharth. You know everything about me. Mother is alone and there is no one else for her apart from me. You know the way she brought me up amidst all the difficulties and the time has come for me to pay back in gratitude. If I abandon her, it will not be fair and Allah won't forgive me, Siddharth," said Imran.

"How can you imagine me saying you to leave your mother? She will be with us and will have everything she has in Hyderabad. Nothing will delight her more than this place. Peaceful atmosphere, pollution-less air, you, me, Swetha, what else does she need? You know how much she likes the company of Swetha," said Siddharth.

"She will definitely be very much delighted to come here. If you ask her to come, there is no way she denies your request but my point is different. You know everything, the way she brought me up, the difficulties she had to face without my dad. Now I have grown up and it is the time for me to look after her. I want to provide her comfortable life and don't want her to be in difficulties amidst our struggle for a change. Nasreen's dad too will never agree for this and will not let her marry me," said Imran and added, "I hope you understand my intentions, Siddharth. I have more priorities in life than to fight for the change of the world."

"That's okay, Imran."

Akanksha, who was listening to the conversation,

interfered and asked, "Why does everyone like Swetha so much? What is the magic in her that everyone gets attracted to her so much?"

"Swetha is the most mature, understanding, and down-to-earth girl I have ever met in my life. Her smile, worth a million, can mesmerize anyone. A real sweet heart and a very caring person whom you can trust without any hesitation. She is the best listener I have come across. Whatever be it, she listens with complete interest and always gives respect to others feelings and thoughts, makes everyone feel that she is the best pal ever," said Imran.

"If you observed her keenly, there is always a smile in her eyes even when she doesn't smile, which makes her clearly distinct from others," said Siddharth.

"How did you happen to like her?"

"That's a long story. Do you want to know about it?"

"With pleasure."

"Okay then. I will tell you everything since I love telling it. Her father was my teacher. He was not just a teacher for me but more like a guide and a mentor to me. His breadth is wide; his thoughts are far-reaching. It was because of him I used to go to her place frequently. Swetha also studied in my class but I never knew her much. I used to hear from people that she was arrogant and adamant. She never used to talk to anyone. She taught the lower-class students and earned money on her own to help the children in an orphanage... might be because of the fact that she had lost her mother at a very young age. She had a world of her own and used to be busy in it. She rarely talked to me and used to glare angrily at me. I knew that she was jealous of me for I used to top the class and was the leader of the class. All these attributes in her made her look different and soon I began to develop interest in her. It was not any sort of crush but a deep desire to know about her. I tried to smile at her whenever I came across her but she never responded. I tried to create opportunities to talk to her without any positive outcome. Very soon, my visits to her house increased and I found her behaving normally with her dad. She used to joke and tease him. Once I got a chance to be with her. She was talking but I couldn't hear anything and all I could observe was her lips move and eye brows tilt as she talked. Most impressive was the way she brought her tongue while keeping her eyes closed whenever she joked or teased. That mere sight haunted me and did not leave my dreams for the next few days.

As days passed, she started to talk to me and unknowingly I was drawn to her. Everytime we met, she gave a wonderful smile that would shake my heart. In the school, she used to talk only to me as if I were her closest pal. She used to be so concerned and convincing in her manners that I used to fall in love everytime I talked to her. But it was not the end. As every love story has got its own problem, mine too got its own. Occasionally, when the situation demanded, she used to talk to a few other boys. They would be laughing while talking and I used to bite my nails till the conversation ended. I didn't know what was going on in her mind, but whenever she talked to someone, I would feel so jealous and soon I realized that my competitors grew. My relationship with other boys who talked to her frequently soured. But I knew from some corner of my heart that I am special for her and I had my own logic for it. She never started a conversation with anyone on her own except me. Whenever she saw someone she would just smile but in my case, the smile starts from the eyes. Maybe those were all my presumptions, I don't know, but the fact is that there were serious competitors for me competing for her. The stage of impressing which I think would come to everyone in their life had entered my life too. I had one advantage over others. I was close to her dad and through him I happened to get some valuable information about her. Her favorite color was blue and so most of my T shirts were blue. I talked about panipuri all the time, for she liked it more than anything else. She was a singer and I used to listen to the songs she used to sing. She gave importance to lyrics and every time we talked about songs, I used to bring the topics of her favorite lyricists Veturi and Cinare in the conversation. Though she was a classical singer and dancer, she was quite modern in her appearance and thoughts. She is a Christian but sings mostly Hindu classical songs.

When I asked her about her favorite book, she told it was 'Glimpses of World History' which her father presented to her. Most of the time, she talked about civilizations and the people. I knew that her father was behind all this but all these sorts of things from a girl interested me. All the other girls whom I knew talked about Katrina Kaif and Bollywood. When you hear history from a girl, history sounds wonderful. The mysteries in her always attracted me and everyday was a continuous process of knowing her. I used to have utmost satisfaction when I was with her. I wanted to convey all my feelings but as soon as I saw her, I used to become hesitant and landed up not telling her.

The comparison might not be appropriate but I cannot co-relate my journey with her better than this. I realized she was like a vast mountain with various difficult paths to go through initially. But as you move further, your anxiety and the curiosity increase as the paths become interesting and when you reach the top, it is where you can really feel her and cannot afford to lose her. The soothing effect the cool breeze creates there is beyond description. It can only be felt," said Siddharth.

"That was wonderful. So you had a very good childhood because of Swetha. Mine was very boring. When I look back for my childhood memories, all I can see is the boarding school and the tuitions," said Akanksha.

"Imran's childhood is lot better than mine. Both Nasreen and Imran are looking at each other since childhood. It's just looking at each other and nothing more than that," said Siddharth as he smiled.

"When and how did you propose Swetha," asked Akanksha as if she was not interested in Imran's story.

"In one of the math class, she came and asked me about a topic called 'limit.' It is then I got the opportunity to tell her," and when he was about to tell it, Akanksha said "Experiencing the Limit! Isn't it?"

"How do you know it? Did Surya tell it to you?" asked Siddharth.

"No, Swetha told me. But tell me, how did you come up with that idea?"

"The moment I thought about her, thoughts flooded my mind but I wanted my proposal to be different and was thinking about it for quite some time. I was young but it is Swetha and so I didn't care about anything else. One day, the day of my luck, one inspector came to college and asked questions for which every student stood up in vain unable to answer. Then was the turn of Swetha. She had worst nightmares about math and that day was no exception. That inspector randomly put her many questions though she couldn't answer any. Swetha who got a bit irritated said, "It is difficult to answer, if they come in a random way. I doubt whether you will be able to answer if questions are asked so randomly considering the fact that the time given to answer is also very less." The surprised inspector then said, "Okay, as you wish. Let me give you two days. Isn't it enough? Three days! Four days! Okay, I give you one week which I think is more than what you need. I restrict just to the starting chapter 'limit' and let me see the way you answer the questions from it. The same day you can ask me any question in entire math and see whether I can answer you or not."

The inspector left and people called her arrogant again. She might be so but I wouldn't have got the courage to talk the way she did and that moment I liked her the most and learnt from her the most. That day she studied hard. If it would have been any other subject, she would have handled well but it was mathematics, so she was frightened. On her father's advice, she came to ask me and I explained it to her in the best way I could.

The next day, I wanted to tell her all my feelings by witnessing the courage with which she talked to the inspector. I thought of putting everything I felt about her on a paper. Thoughts flooded about her as soon as I began but I wanted to make it special and so I thought very much about it until an idea crept into my mind. I thought of explaining my feelings in the form of 'limit.' The inspector didn't come but he praised Swetha for her courage in front of my principal who was very much delighted and presented her a pen.

I liked the inspector for my own reasons. It was because of his arrival that I could tell her all my feelings. She took a long time to reply but I could tell her that I liked her more than anything else.

Then Imran said, "Swetha is really the best thing we have in our life. She would be there with us all the time. She knows how to make people happy. She cares a lot for my mother. She always would tell my mother something about me and make her laugh. She is half responsible for my mother's health. My mother would never allow me to marry a girl other than a Muslim but if it was the case with Swetha, she would definitely allow me and that is applicable to everyone who knows her. All the artificial boundaries like the religion, race and caste have to tumble down for her."

"Yeah, I also observed the same. Surya's dad, who is a caste-maniac, also likes Swetha very much," said Akanksha.

Siddharth said, "Swetha and Surya like each other and they forget the world when they are together. Their girls versus boys debates are always interesting to watch."

"I wish I were Swetha," said Akanksha and continued, "I came here to pass some time but now I realize what life is. Every person is unique in his or her own way and is contributing in one way or other to me."

11
CHAPTER

The First Night

The room was fully decorated with flowers and a number of varieties of fruits were placed on the table by the side of the bed which was flooded with lilies. Its sweet flavor embraced every corner of the room. The atmosphere was calm, seductive and would force every heart to unlock its romantic doors. The doors were closed and Surya sat on the bed wearing a traditional dhoti. He was very much tensed thinking about the future course of action that was to take place.

Just then, there was a knock on the door and Surya could hear some female voices. His tension peaked and not knowing what do to, he sat firmly as the door opened. There was exchange of words just outside the door which he couldn't make out and all of a sudden, the girl, in a traditional sari, was pushed inside by her mischievous friends. The doors were shut again. Both their hearts started beating fast and there was complete silence for the next few seconds. The girl went back to lock the door and started to walk slowly towards Surya keeping her head down, holding a glass of milk in her hands.

Her loyal slow walk reduced Surya's tension and as she approached him, he moved aside to give her space to sit. She sat beside him silently keeping her head down, moved her hand with the glass of milk towards him indicating him to drink the milk. Surya took the glass and kept it on the desk which was positioned beside him.

She slowly raised her voice and said, "Don't keep the glass there. I brought it for you. You drink half the glass and give me the other half."

"Leave it. I just want to talk to you," he said and continued, "What is your name? I am sorry but I have to tell you. The marriage was fixed without my knowledge."

"Did I do something wrong?" she said as tears rolled down her cheeks.

"You, mad girl. What are you crying for? You didn't do anything wrong. My intention is just to tell you everything the way it happened. I never wanted to marry this way but my dad doesn't listen to me. That is the reason why I didn't even know your name and see your picture. This is the only way I thought I could change my dad's views. He always wanted me to marry a girl of same caste and status and he never bothered to know my likings."

She didn't speak.

Surya said, "Will you tell me your name or should I keep calling you mad girl for the rest of our married life?"

She smiled sweetly with her lips rubbing against each other due to the friction generated by the long silence and, like a child, said, "My name is Anitha."

He moved his hand around her chin, raised her face, cleared the tears on her face and looking directly into her eyes said, "Don't be afraid. I am just like one of your friends."

Her eyes still looking into his eyes now trembled and at once she closed her eyes indicating her agreement for his proposal.

"What did you study?" he said.

"I studied till seventh standard. I can read and write Telugu. I have learnt some English words for you."

"Is it?"

"Yeah, shall I tell them?"

"Yes, tell me."

"You are good boy and I like you," said she with a smile thinking that she has impressed him a bit.

"Why did you learn English for me?"

"Everyone speaks English now-a-days. So, I thought that would impress you."

"I like Telugu more than anything else. When Telugu is spoken by an innocent one like you, it is even most pleasant to hear," said Surya and added, "By the way, do you know anything about me? What did your parents tell about me?"

"They told me that you hail from a good family, were well-educated and advised me to listen to whatever you say. They told me to support you always and warned me not to contradict you as you are well-educated and know better than me. They told me I am very lucky to become your wife."

"Lucky! For what?"

"You don't drink and smoke. You are educated and good-looking. What else does a girl need? I have a friend named Ramya who got married last year. Her husband is from the same caste but later on, she found to her horror that he is an alcoholic. Every night he drinks and beats her insisting for extra dowry. She always cries telling this whenever she comes to me. She advised me to marry a person who is not a drunkard even if he is not from the same caste."

"I don't drink. That's okay. But what if I am not a good guy?"

"Those things, I think I can take care of by being good to you. My mother always told me that every person's behavior is a reflection of our own behavior. So, by being good and faithful to you, I thought I can change you but in other cases, like the habit of drinking, it is very difficult. Almost every male in my village is addicted to alcohol and at night they come and beat their wives. I talk to some of them. Most of them are very good and talk like saints in the morning but at night, some demon enters them and they behave like monsters. While choosing the match, my father's aim was to find someone who doesn't drink from our caste. By God's grace I got you."

They began to have refreshments.

"Did you prepare all these items?" said Surya.

"No, my mother did. Do you like them?"

"Yeah, they are very tasty," said Surya.

After Surya was done with his meal, Anitha came forward to take the plate to clean it. Surya stopped her from taking the plate and said, "Please remember that you are my wife and not a servant."

"I don't feel like a servant. Being your wife, I find pleasure in doing it. My mother cleaned my father's and my grandmother cleaned grandfather's plate. I don't feel good if someone else cleans it," she said.

"It's up to you. If you find pleasure in it, I won't force you. But at any point of time, if you feel it as a burden or feel like not doing it, don't do it. Just don't consider it as your duty."

Anitha took the plate, cleaned it, placed in the kitchen and returned back to find Surya on the bed.

"Do you watch movies?"

"I watch them on television. There is no theatre in my village. To go to the town, I have to go with my father but he is always busy and doesn't allow me to go with someone else. I have watched only two movies in my life. When my grandfather died, as per our custom, we were not supposed to sleep on the 10th day. So we went for a movie. The other was when I was in school... the school management took us for a movie but I have always wanted to see movies in theatres. Watching big stars on the big screen while people are whistling and clapping is real fun. People always talk about the thrill of watching Chiranjeevi movie on the first day. When my grandfather died, we went to *Choodalani undi*. When Chiru was dancing, I almost felt like standing up and whistling."

Surya smiled and said, "Don't worry about that, Anitha. I am a movie buff and I will take you regularly to movies. I will see that you watch all the Chiranjeevi movies at least within the first three days of release."

"Thank you very much!"

"What else do you like which was forbidden in your house?" asked Surya.

"Why do you ask me so many questions?" enquired Anitha.

"It is out of curiosity. It interests me. Moreover I liked your voice. Do you sing?"

"Yeah, since childhood, we grew up viewing all the dramas. Every day, good devotional songs would be played in temple and I used to hear them. One day, I sang in my school and my headmaster was so impressed that, as a reward, he gave me a CD of S Janaki songs and made me sing in the temple in front of everybody."

"Have you not tried to sing in any singing programs on television?"

"When I watch the singing programs on television, I always feel like singing there but nobody allows me in my house to cross the village limits for things like these. They might do so in cities but for us, the television programs are only for viewing purpose."

"Your voice is like that of a bird's voice in a desert and no one is there to hear you. I will try to expose it to the real world."

"I don't understand what you are telling ," said Anitha.

"It doesn't matter but tell me one thing. How many times did you leave your village?"

"There was no need to leave the village. We get most of the things here and so I have never left the village except on special occasions when all the family members had to go. I am a girl and so they never allowed me to go alone or with my friends. But I managed to go to town a few times. It is very difficult there with all the buses and the traffic but there is life everywhere in the town and is really good. My friends are congratulating me because I will move to Hyderabad with you. I have seen Charminar and Tank Bund only in television. I feel I'm very lucky to marry you as most of my dreams are going to come true."

Surya was moved and remained silent unable to speak after hearing all that she said.

"What happened? Why are you not speaking?" asked Anitha.

"Nothing, I was just thinking about something."

"Shall I ask you one thing? You should be frank and should not lie at any cost..."

"Yeah, sure..."

"Do you like me now?"

"Yes, of course. I like you very much. And, do you like me?"

"I liked you the moment I saw your picture. Since then, I had many sleepless nights thinking about you. You were in my dreams all the time. I like you more in real now than in my dreams. When I talked to you now, I liked you even more. You are more than my expectations and I am very much satisfied. I was desperate to see you during the marriage and nothing else was in my mind. I moved my head back and forth and, in the process, had the glimpses of you many times."

"It's not just you who was trying to get the glimpses. I also tried as much as I could. The first thing I noticed was your hand which was trembling. I felt like placing my hand on yours to give you enough strength. Do you remember the moment the elder women came forward to reduce the gap between us? Both our shoulders touched in the process and I didn't want to move them away. I tried as much as I could to maintain our contact and enjoyed those few minutes very much."

"I too loved the touch and pushed you with my shoulder. You might have noticed it..." said Anitha.

"Yeah, I noticed it. It is then I got enough courage and had a look at you. The moment I saw you, I was lost. Those beautiful eyes revealed everything that you were expecting from me and has taken me to some sort of dreamy world where only you and I are there," said Surya.

"I too went to some sort of dreamy world after I saw you."

"Let's hope that the dream world which we could see becomes true," said Surya.

"I love you very much."

"Me too, Anitha."

"What do you like the most in me?"

"There are many things, my dearest Anitha..."

"Did you like my eyes?"

"Very much till I could hear you speak. Now I like your voice."

"You mean to say that the first place goes to my voice and then the eyes. What else do you like?"

"I like this nose, the curvy tiny nose and then your lips. I love your lips when they move slowly. The moment you entered the room, you were very silent and when I asked you to speak you moved your lips very slowly. It was so tempting."

"Do you want me to move my lips like that again?"

"I would die for that."

"I'm not able to do that now."

"It comes when you are angry with me."

"Then, I guess, you can't see it again."

"Is it so? Let us see what happens in future."

"What else do you like in me?"

"Then, I like your little tongue that you hide inside most of the time."

Anitha brought out the tongue a little and began to laugh.

"A little more," said Surya.

"No, I can't," said Anitha with a smile and added, "Tell me something else. What else do you like?"

"I liked everything that I have seen in you. Every tiny little part of yours, your eyes, eyebrows, ears, hair, nose, tongue, lips and the neck."

"What else do you want to see?" said she as she moved close towards him.

"Everything that you want to show me," said Surya, catching her hands.

The questionnaire continued and both of them came to know each other until they forgot the fact that they were strangers till the previous day and came together to become one.

12

The Campaign Begins

"India is a poor third world country, they say. Let them call the way they want. For us, India is not a poor country but is a country with many poor people living in it. The people are also poor just in the context of money. Wealth is concentrated in the hands of a very few and we are all here anticipating some changes. What shall we do then? Shall we kill those very few and distribute the wealth equally among all? It might be okay for a year or 10 years or, say, 50 years. What happens again? The exploiter begins to exploit the ignorant again and the world will be same again. So we are not going to forests to kill that few. We are all human beings and we know the value of life and so we choose the path that is human. At the same time, we should be aware of the human greediness and his will to satisfy his desires and ego. What shall we do then? We think before we act, target the main reasons for all these conditions and see that anything we do would benefit in the long run. Yes, it is ignorance of opportunities and lack of education. We try to educate them and let them know the way world is. This might take some months, in fact, some years, but let's start it. Let's not stick to the virtual world of debates or editorials. Instead, we should come to the real world where the change really is required and we do this with full heart. The fruit of serving others is very sweet. When you change somebody and he or she realizes the reason as you, it is then you understand the full meaning of your life. All the narrowness in us widens embracing all sorts of things both living and non-living, making us broad. The happiness we get by living in a society, which is fully harmonious with us, is second to none.

Once again, I remind you. The rich are only rich till the poor are ignorant. The moment the poor realizes this, the pillars of the rich tumble down and when he falls down, he has to learn living on the ground. This applies anywhere whether in a village or a town or a country or in the world. Nobody is bound to be the rich forever.

Now I have decided to contribute my part in utilizing the potential of the poor, make them aware of other options and most importantly educate them. This has to be done by the government but what if the government cashes in on the ignorance of the people. We are students and we have a purpose. We can't stay looking at the conditions of this kind. I have decided to start with a village to do some meaningful activities there and I would be delighted if someone who wants to do some meaningful work accompanies me," said Siddharth.

Thus, Siddharth completed his speech and came down the steps. The crowd was large enough and most of them were students with similar aims whom Siddharth had gathered since his college days. Some thought the speech as electrifying, some felt it was foolish, some thought it as an exaggeration of facts, some felt bored but nevertheless there were good discussions and debates going on in the premises.

Siddharth came near Surya and asked, "Hello Surya. How is Anitha? How are things going on?"

"Everything is fine and your speech was very good. I want to tell you many things and I will tell them later. I know that you are planning to leave at the earliest, but please wait for a few more days for my sake. I also asked Akanksha to wait till *Ganesh Nimajjanam*. You know what this festival means to us."

"Why are you requesting me idiot? Just, command me and I have to obey it. Even Swetha will be delighted to see *Nimajjanam*."

13

Ganesh Nimajjanam

Lord Ganesha is placed in an open auditorium for nine days and is worshipped by everyone. This festival is a pleasure for children, heaven for youth and the beginning of an auspicious time for old. The time has come for Ganesha to be immersed in the water and everyone is eagerly waiting for the moment.

Surya, Siddharth, Imran, Swetha, Akanksha and Anitha gathered before the Ganesha. The idol was about six-feet high. Ganesha was sitting on his vehicle — the rat — and his favorite laddu was placed in one of his many hands.

People were having their final prayers. The local MLA was invited to break the coconut. Amidst full cheering, the coconut was broken and a truck decorated with palm leaves was brought near the stage where Ganesha was present. All the young men came forward to lift the idol shouting loudly the slogan "Ganpathi *bappa morya* , *ada ladoo* choriya. Jai bolo Ganesh maharaj ki jai."

They slowly lifted the idol and managed to put it safely on the truck. Surrounded by the waving palm trees, Ganesha was looking more beautiful now. Then the most awaited music of the drum band started. Young children, who were already on cloud nine, started dancing to famous Bollywood tunes of the band and the parents were extremely delighted to look at their children dance. At a corner place, the youth sat to have their fast drinks and everyone drank in a hurry. A big can full of *prasad* was brought and was placed in the truck on the rear end. With the signal received from the purohit for the auspicious timing, the truck started moving. At the rear side, the *prasad* was being given and so the children all of a sudden rushed there. Now that the truck had started moving, the youth placed a ribbon around their fore-head and went forward. A few of them who were already drunk started dancing as the beats of *teen maar* and *dho maar* repeated while the truck moved at a speed of less than 10 meter per hour.

Two young fellows in the dancing crowd signalled Surya to come and join them. As Surya shied away, they came near him and pulled him into the crowd. He was reluctant to dance initially but at the insistence of his friends, he started dancing amidst much cheer. Anitha couldn't stop laughing seeing her husband dance. When someone gets into the vibe of the dancing crowd, what happens to him all of a sudden, one may not know, but the desi beats always has this inherent capability to evoke a stunning extemporaneous dance performance. As Surya was burning the dance floor, a 100-rupee note was placed between his lips. Seeing the note, the music band performed even better, forcing the crowd to go crazy. The note was finally removed from Surya's mouth and was given to the leader of the band as a sign of appreciation for their excellent drum beats.

The truck moved a few more meters and stopped again. Now it was the turn of Siddharth as Surya didn't want to leave Siddharth alone. He wanted Siddharth to join the dance. The cheering time for Swetha had come. Siddharth, in order to avoid dancing, started to run away from the crowd but the crowd managed to catch him and forced him to go to the dancing zone. Siddharth was not a dancer but due to the pressure of the crowd, he had to dance. The moment he designed a dance step, Swetha burst out with laughter. Surya, who was already in a full swing, removed a 500 rupee note and placed it between the lips of Siddharth which raised Sidharth's passion to dance and the note finally moved to the pockets of the band leader as the tempo of the music went high.

The truck moved very slowly, remaining halt for most of the time. The truck stopped once again and this time, most of the youth, including Siddharth and Surya, moved aside giving way to Imran. Imran was a good dancer and his street dance during removal of idols had earned him an immense fan following in his neighborhood.

"Why did Imran go there all of a sudden?" enquired Akanksha.

"Wait and see the magic," said Swetha as Imran removed a knife from his pocket and started swaying the knife with his body moving synchronously to the motion of knife. Amidst full whistles and claps, Imran was desperately trying to show his full talent. The truck almost stayed put for 20 minutes and wouldn't move further.

"What is the magic? I am not able to understand a bit," said Akanksha

"Try to observe Imran's eyes while dancing or the moment he stops dancing for a second and you are sure to understand the magic," said Swetha.

Akanksha, now her attention fully concentrated on Imran, found that he was frequently observing a girl on the top floor in front of the house where he was dancing.

"I think you have found out the magic that is forcing Imran to dance that way. It is Nasreen, his childhood sweet heart. Observe her carefully. The moment she smiles at him, you can feel the reaction here in Imran," said Swetha.

"Yeah, she is smiling looking at him and he is completely lost in her smile," said Akanksha.

Then Surya pulled Imran back from the dancing zone and said, "Your heroine has watched you for a long time. Now give turn to others so that they can impress their loved ones."

Imran gave a quick look at the top floor and Nasreen gave a smile. He then looked at Surya and said, "*Teri maaki*, you are married already. What do you know about the pain of singles?"

Thus the truck moved slowly halting at all strategic points where one could easily locate a young boy desperately trying to grab the attention of the crowd though his main intention was to grab the attention of the person he intends to. One could also observe a girl standing at some corner witnessing the young boy trying to woo her attention.

After passing through all the strategic love points and increasing the intimacy between the love birds, Ganesha finally managed to reach the Tank Bund where he was to be immersed. After staying in queue for a long time, Ganesha was immersed along with his fellow idols. While coming back, everyone felt the loneliness and the memories that Ganesha had left behind. Finally, they reached the same auditorium from which Ganesha was lifted while some people moved away to their places.

Siddharth, Swetha, Surya, Imran and Akanksha reached the stage from where Ganesha was removed which was now full of flowers and decorations.

"How do you feel Akanksha?" asked Swetha.

"I really cannot describe my feelings. It is really mind-boggling and one of the best moments I had. I never thought India would be so beautiful and now I understand what to be an Indian is. People here are living in such happiness in spite of all the miseries they have. It is really an eye-opener for me," said Akanksha, a bit emotionally.

"Yes, indeed people are happy here in spite of the fact that they don't even have the basic requirements. I don't understand how the people here have got the strength and the will power. I am sorry Siddharth since I have never tried to understand your point," said Surya, while everyone stared at him in astonishment.

"*Teri maaki*, what happened to you all of a sudden?"

"Seriously Surya! Today you sound like Siddharth. What happened to you all of a sudden?" said Swetha.

"Anitha is responsible for all the changes in me. The first time I talked to her, I felt very humbled. How can a girl be that way? She is so pious and innocent. Her village is her world and she has never watched a film with her friends. All these restrictions are because of the fact that she is a girl. The moment I showed her the Charminar, you should have seen the child in her, the glow in her face and the happiness in her that she could see something which she watched so far only on television. I can't imagine how happy she would feel if I take her to Taj Mahal or the Eiffel Tower. She treats me as an incarnation of God since I treat her equal, don't drink and beat her. See the expectations with which she has grown up and the happiness she is deriving from the most obvious things. What would have been her condition if she would have been given in hand to some crooked fellow whose sole purpose is to exploit his wife. It is not just the case of Anitha; it is the case with almost every girl in the villages. I felt like crying for all that she had told me with utter innocence. Even then, Siddharth, I am not ready to come with you as I have made up my mind to give her happiness that she has lost all her life. I want to give meaning to her meaningless life so far and show her what life really is like. The moment I feel that I have given at least some meaning to her life, I will not come alone, but with her... not the same Anitha, but a completely transformed Anitha who knows her rights, who challenges the pitfalls in the society and an Anitha, who would lead the women of her kind for rest of her life."

By hearing these intense words from Surya, everybody was touched. Everyone remained silent and tears almost rolled down Swetha's eyes.

"This particular moment, your words have filled the void in me. It has given me enough strength to move further. Now nothing in the world would stop me until I myself perish," said Siddharth.

When it was almost early in the morning, Surya and Akanksha thought of leaving.

"Tomorrow is your flight isn't it? Don't forget us, Akanksha," said Siddharth.

"How can I forget someone from whom I have learnt the true meaning of life? I don't know how I came but now I leave as a person with never-fading memories of you guys that gave color to my life. All these days with you guys are the most memorable days in my life and I can never forget them. The Charminar, Afzalgunj, the beautiful Indian villages, Ganesha and his love pairs, how much could I experience in so little time. Thank you for nurturing the seeds of true happiness in me and giving me the required strength to make it blossom. Swetha and Siddharth, especially, the marks you have engraved on my heart will never get destroyed in my lifetime. I will be in contact with all of you. By the time I come back again, I wish Imran to be married with Nasreen. Love you all guys. Have a very good future," Akanksha in an emotional tone.

CHAPTER 14

The Unrecognised Potential

After three months

Dear Surya,

How are you? How is Anitha? Hope both of you are fine and doing well.

Things are fine here but the pace at which they are moving is very slow. Initially, it was very difficult convincing people what my intentions were. They had mistaken me for a young politician in search of votes but as days proceeded, they grew the confidence in me. Last week, a few of Anitha's friends came to meet me and Swetha. With their help, we talked to a few of the educated in the village and it was a big relief. Then we crossed the village that was supposed to be Anitha's world. You know, Anitha's world was just a radius of two kilometers after which there is a town. Luckily, we could find a railway colony where we got the opportunity to meet the retired railway employees. We talked to them and they have shown keen interest in our work. We went to all the old age homes in the town and talked with them too. On the whole, things are moving very well and the villagers have gained some faith in our work. We are planning for a grand meeting after a month. I will update you soon with the results.

Regards,
Siddharth

After a year
Dear Surya,
Received your letter last week. Good to hear that you are happy there. What was Anitha's reaction after she saw the Taj Mahal?

Things are fine here. The meeting, on which we had high hopes, can now be called a success. People's faith on us has increased immensely and around 1000 people attended it. We realized that the time has come for us to proceed further.

Many people have got a lot of potential which can fetch them whatsoever they desire but most of them are either jobless or depend on agriculture for their sustenance.

We have hired two language translators, two editors and have come to an understanding with a publisher whose sole purpose is not profit. We are encouraging both the literate and the illiterate to pen down or express their thoughts. We are reminding them of their wealth the grand old civilization has given them in the form of beautiful village songs, the great old myths, the village temple debates, the dramas etc. We are making them realize their potential that remains completely unutilized. It was very hard to make them understand all these but we are trying our level best. We then translated the books, edited and published them. Many books were written and around 10 books were published.

You might have heard the book called, 'Village, my mother' which was an instant success. It was written by an old man in Telugu and later it was translated to other languages. It is sort of an autobiography. Till now, there were only autobiographies of famous men and women but here is one of a poor villager which has caught the attention of the public. He has written it wonderfully and as you read it, every sentence bears testimony to the hard

circumstances under which he has grown up amidst
struggles. He has penned down his memories in a
beautiful fashion. It has many of his memories like the
pleasure he got the first time he held his newly-born
daughter in his hands and his worry when a daughter
was born for the second time. He elaborates the love and
care with which he has brought up his son at the expense
of his daughters who finally sent him out of his house,
forcing him to live in an old age home. He then explains
about his lonely journey in the village when everyone has
left him behind. He has penned down all this feelings
perfectly and it was an instant success. As its success grew,
the other books too are gaining their own prominence.

With the profit we gained, we performed the marriages
of some village girls who were in need of money. Literate
men want dowries and there is no way they marry without
a dowry for all the money that was invested on them with
the dowries in mind. Nevertheless, it doesn't matter as the
village drunkards have no option now than to stop drinking
in case they want to have a wife.

We have also opened a school where some retired
employees teach. Swetha teaches the illiterate women. The
entire village likes Swetha very much and calls her
"Swethamma (Mother Swetha)." When an old woman
asked her what the meaning of government was, Swetha
didn't have an answer as there is no government institute
or government agency here in this village.

Almost all the boys swim exceptionally well here and
you definitely might have known about this. With much
difficulty we selected five of them and took them to the
competitions where one among them was selected for the
district team. The coach assured that he would definitely
reach greater heights and he would see to it that he gets
good sponsors. The boy's parents couldn't understand
how swimming could be a source of income. They should
have known that swimming could be a career. Anyway,
better late than never...

Once, we took the picture of a smiling tribal old woman
and sent it to a magazine with the tagline as 'The tribal smile,
our wealth.' The photograph got an instant popularity and

when rewarded, the entire village was shocked to know how money can be earned in so many ways.

You might remember the boy Chiru who sold us amlas on our way to your wedding. He is with us right now and is studying in our school. His sister is learning classical dance. That little girl, who spoke to us in sweet broken voice, has started speaking now and you would really love to hear her speak. We got their dad, who used to torture his mother, arrested. But the mother pleaded with the police to leave him alone. I don't understand how she is able to love her husband in spite of all his tortures.

We have recorded a few songs sung by the children in the form of cassettes. It didn't fetch any result as the marketing was poor from our side. One day, two boys came to beg along with a cow which had a bell tied around her neck. They sang in order to beg for food. There was lot of lyrical content with soothing music and we happened to record their voice which became an instant success. They will be performing in Hyderabad next month.

Thus there are many talents that are unexposed and go unrecognized because of ignorance and lack of education. It is just because they don't know that there are other things to do. Left with no option, all the village children either go after the buffaloes or remain jobless thinking that a messiah will come to save their lives. We will try our level best to expose the potential that is unutilized. There will be many hurdles too but we will do as much as we can. So far, I have been mentioning only about the successes we have seen. There were many failures too but everything was an experience and we have gained enough courage to move ahead with all the support received from the people. Three inter caste marriages were made. It was very hard and there was a lot of opposition for it but somehow we could convince the people. Along with appreciation, opposition is also growing. Will update you with the results.

After three months
Dear Surya,
Imran is coming here along with his mother. Nasreen

has told about Imran to her parents and so we can expect their marriage soon. Swetha is very much excited about their marriage.

Things are fine here. Our recognition is surging along with the opposition. The standard of living of the people here is changing for the better. Last week, an American organization recognised our good work and agreed to give 10 lakh rupees as fund. One of our village boys is a contestant on a music show on television. You might have heard about Chandu, as he is pretty famous now. Last time, I told you about a boy who was selected in the district swimming team. He is now in the State swimming team and two others got selected in the district team. It is very good to witness the achievements of these young ones.

I want you to come here as soon as possible. There are signs of my decay. Last week, a gang of a local politician came here and gave me a warning. Their problem is strange. Now that we are educating people in schools, they fear that they might lose their votes as the voters might opt for an eligible candidate. But this is not going to stop me from continuing my work. Yesterday they came again, slapped me and warned me. I feel this one is not a simple warning. I am very much worried about Swetha. She would be left alone without me. I don't have any fear about the work. Everyday our strength is increasing as people are coming to join us from various parts of the country. They can kill me but not everyone. For every person they kill, there are hundreds and hundreds who are going to join. But as I said earlier, my worry is about Swetha. She will be fine if you are there with her. Hope to see you soon.

Regards,
Siddharth

After two days
Siddharth was sitting on the steps of the front room and called Swetha who was watering the plants. As she came and sat beside him, he looked deep into her eyes, hugged her and started to weep like a child. His voice trembled, unable to utter a word. He hugged her tight

and said with a trembling voice, "I love you, Swetha. I love you very much."

Swetha sensing his strange behavior said, "What happened, Siddharth?"

"I am just worrying about you, Swetha. Every day, I get bad dreams where I leave you behind and go somewhere very far. I sometimes wonder why I have chosen this. I would have given you a wonderful life if we were in Hyderabad. I brought you here where you are forced to live without any comforts and have to work hard every day amidst difficulties. See the plight of Jayaprakash Narayan. In spite of his sincere efforts to do service to people, no one is listening to him. What Surya said was right. People come and go, revolutions come and go, but people and their lives remain the same. It was foolish of me to think of the change."

"What is more comfortable to me than staying with you, Siddharth? You are very tired and so you get all these bad dreams. You just need to take some rest. You are not realizing what you have been achieving. You have started a new era and the entire country is witnessing your deeds. You have brought about these changes right from the grassroots level. Yesterday, there was an article in *Eenadu* about our work. Lots of people are getting to know about your work. Any work done with a good heart will never perish. If people like you lose heart, there is nothing that can change the world," said Swetha as she rested her head on Siddharth's shoulders.

Then they heard a bird sing. It was for a very short period and there was silence again. The bird started singing again, this time for a greater duration. After hearing the bird sing, another bird came towards it and now both of them started to sing bringing their beaks together.

"Did you hear it?" asked Swetha.

"What?"

"The birds singing."

"Yes, it is very delightful to hear."

"Do you know why birds sing here and not in the city?"

"Since they find everything in sync with the nature right?"

"Yes, it could find everything here that it couldn't find it in the city. Nature in sync with her and her lover beside her and so her heart couldn't wait to sing," said Swetha and both of them hugged each other tight.

The next day

"How did this happen?" asked Surya with a broken voice with Anitha beside him.

Swetha was sitting beside the body of Siddharth dumbstruck. She looked like a body that had lost its soul.

Surya went near the body, sat on his knees and yelled, "Siddharth! My dearest friend! You asked me to come as soon as possible and so I have come here for you. Why have you left me, dear? Open your eyes for my sake," and he wept like a child.

The entire village had tears rolling down their cheeks now that their beloved guide had left them for ever. Small children unaware of the meaning of death came to their loving brother and tried to wake him up. The media arrived at the scene. People from various organizations rushed to the village as soon as they heard the news. Many students came to see the departure of their leader.

Swetha, with her face fully swollen, now stood up and tried to speak something but was unable to. With much difficulty, she started to speak but burst into tears again. The media came forward to concentrate on what she was going to tell. She somehow managed to clear her throat and said, "The spring has just begun but the singing bird has gone very far... to never return back. A few people came and hit him with an axe... they must be the men of the village politician. He didn't die as soon as he was hit... there was life left in him for some moments. Even in those last moments, he was thinking about you and me. You might be knowing of his recorder with which he has been recording songs of our village children. He has recorded his last wishes in the same recorder," said Swetha as tears flooded her eyes. Surya came forward, hugged her and then switched on the recorder.

"My dear brothers and sisters, my time has come now and it is time for me to leave all of you. We have started this movement with a lot of effort and it should not come to an abrupt end because of my departure. They have hurt me out of their ignorance... they might hurt someone else again but that should not affect our work. We are also not going to take any revenge. We are all human beings and we know the value of life. They might kill one or two but they can never kill our ideology. Our growing light of the candle should not be put off by the mild wind blown by them. Please look after my Swetha. She is a girl with immense strength and without me, she might lose all her strength. All of you should become her strength. My friends Surya and Imran will be coming soon with very valuable suggestions for you. Please receive them well. Being a Hindu, I believe in rebirth. I hope my next birth is not going to determine my fate... I don't want that to happen to any other child in this world. I pray to God to make this particular wish come true. I think my time has arrived now... take care, Swetha..."

As the voice faded away, the entire village could see the dawn of a revolution... days were never going to be the same again for them.

Pls do spread a word about
the book, if you liked it 🙂

Acknowledgements

Since childhood, I had the habit of analysing things around me in depth but restricted it mostly to sciences. During my college days, I was, all of a sudden, exposed to various genres of movies, literature, drama and other artistic works which increased my horizon of thinking. I developed a deep desire to know more, tried to explore and embrace as many subjects as possible and, in the process, developed some tastes and interests. Literary and artistic achievements anywhere amused me and my mind soon became a fertile ground of fresh thoughts and ideas. This book is a result of my deep desire to write and contribute something towards our society. This work is something that has blossomed from the bottom of my heart.

In the course of writing this novel, I have taken the help of my family members and friends for their comments on various chapters. Among them, I would like to thank my brother Kranthi Kumar, sister Radhika, Gopi Ganesan, Ashutosh Jindal, Shravya Kothapally, Archana and Satheesh Kumar. My special thanks to Sirish Basani who was extremely generous with time and effort, without whose valuable feedback, this book wouldn't have come to this stage. My sincere and humble thanks to Leadstart Publishing and Sunil K Poolani for giving a chance to this amateur writer and enabling my dreams to move to the next level.